CRITICAL CARE

CHENANIAH RIVER
BOOK ONE

STACEY WEEKS

Critical Care

© 2025 Stacey Weeks

ISBN: 978-1-7381668-8-6

MORE FICTION BY STACEY WEEKS

SYCAMORE HILL

To Sweet Beginnings in Sycamore Hill

The Sycamore Standoff

His Sycamore Sweetheart

The Sycamore Slopes

One Sycamore Sunday

A Sycamore Secret

CHENANIAH RIVER

Critical Care

Fatal Homecoming

MISTLETOE MEADOWS

Mistletoe Melody

Mistletoe Mission

Mistletoe Movie Star

STAND ALONE TITLES

The Builder's Reluctant Bride

In Too Deep

This one is for Amanda and Missy.

So, whether you eat or drink, or whatever you do,
do all to the glory of God.

1 Corinthians 10:31

CONTENTS

CHAPTER
ONE

"Bear-be!"

Her son's piercing wail filled the highway rest stop, and not a single person reacted. No surprise there. Abby Sinclair was used to navigating life alone. "It'll be okay, Carson," she shushed. "Mommy will find him."

Her four-year-old curled his arms over his head and grabbed fistfuls of hair. His bright eyes darted wildly about. Abby spun the stroller and retraced their steps, searching for his precious stuffed toy. With three fingers shoved into his slobbery mouth and a feverish pink coloring his chubby cheeks, a meltdown was imminent.

Things were supposed to be better now. The plan had been simple. Leave under the cover of darkness and slip into a new town unnoticed so the trouble didn't follow her. But Carson was just winding up, and there was no way they'd fly under the radar once he let it rip.

The stroller's curved handles moistened under her grip. She didn't need a tantrum cranking up a tension dial already maxed out. She should have left Carson's favorite bear in the car, but she'd been too tired to fight.

"Did you drop him?" Abby faked a happy, bright tone. What kind of mother lost her child's favorite toy? If they lost Bear-be here, they might never find him. Carson would grow up blaming her, not sure why he felt unsafe. But she'd know. Because she couldn't keep track of a simple bear.

Get a grip.

Carson's whimpers increased.

Abby's gaze swept over three closed restaurant fronts and landed on the illuminated open coffee bar and variety shop. Only a handful of people milled about, and none held a bear. In fact, none looked her way, despite Carson's increasing noise. No one seemed to care about a little boy's heartache. She should have kept driving. She would have, except Carson had needed to use the restroom, and she needed a coffee.

The restroom!

She hurried back to the family restroom, but no Bear-be.

Carson's snivels intensified. The only other possibility was that Carson dropped it somewhere between their parking spot and the building. "We'll find him," she promised. "Before Mommy worked in the nursing home, she used to be a police officer, remember? I know all about finding lost things."

Abby rarely spoke of her stint with the police, but she kept up the chatter, embellishing her abilities for entertainment value. She'd only been on the force for five years before changing careers. It still counted, though. And she'd do whatever it took to help Carson feel safe. She was all he had in this world.

And he was all she had.

"Is this what you're looking for?"

Abby spun.

A scruffy man, probably in his early thirties, held out the beloved animal with one hand and hiked up the waistband of his jeans with the other. When he let go of his jeans, they resettled to his hips, exposing the top of his boxers. Dark circles shadowed his bloodshot eyes. Anywhere else, she might have pegged him as homeless, but given their locale, he was likely a long-haul truck driver. Another soul searching for a late-night, caffeinated pick-me-up.

The weight on her chest lifted as she reached for the toy. "Yes! Thank you so much."

Abby leaned around the stroller and handed it to Carson.

Squealing, he clutched it to his chest.

"Carson would have been devastated to lose it," she said to the man. "I appreciate your kindness."

"Carson. That's a nice name." The corners of his lips tipped up, but his eyes scowled. She could have sworn she saw a flicker of recognition in them.

Something about his reaction made the hairs on her neck prickle. *Did her former co-worker send someone after her? She had threatened her, but surely leaving town was sufficient proof she was moving on.*

Abby back-stepped, but kept a smile glued to her face. Five years with the force had taught her to trust her gut. Wanting to believe her apprehension was unwarranted didn't make it true. Instinct had saved her more than once. "Thanks again."

His eyes narrowed. But even if she was overreacting, the guy had to understand why a lone woman at a deserted rest stop would feel uncomfortable talking with a stranger. Off to the side, a police officer served himself a coffee at the self-serve station and wiggled his fingers at Carson.

Her Good Samaritan dipped his head and stepped back. "Have a nice night."

With one eye on the retreating man, Abby resisted the stirrings of guilt. Even if she was wrong, her priority was Carson's safety. It had to be. There was no one else looking out for them.

Abby made herself a coffee and loaded up on snacks. They'd spent the afternoon visiting with her former zone partner Austin Emmerson and his wife Sandy. Maybe the visit had reactivated some suppressed cop-radar that ran under the surface of every person who'd ever worn a badge. She hadn't been a cop for nearly four years, but her instincts remained as strong as ever.

As Abby paid for her purchases, she asked the clerk, "What can you tell me about Chenaniah River?" She'd already done her research, but she liked to hear from the locals.

He shrugged. "Town's pretty quiet. Lots of visitors in the summer 'cause we're so close to the falls, and of course, there's the annual Diamond Festival in February."

"Diamonds?"

"It's an event that brings in nearly as many winter tourists as the summer. One person wins a real diamond every year."

"Sounds exciting," she said with a smile. She hoped they were still here come winter. "Have a good night."

Outside the rest stop in the parking lot, the police officer had her Good Samaritan against the side of an OPP cruiser. The officer stood with his body angled to block escape but not to escalate. Abby slowed her step, keeping her son in sight, and listened.

"—got a tip you've been carrying," the officer said. "And this stop is known for trafficking. Doesn't look good."

The parolee's shoulders tensed. "I wasn't doing nothin' wrong, man. You can't search me."

Abby's pulse ticked faster. She knew that dance. Denial, minimizing, pushing back.

The officer's tone sharpened. "Here's the thing. The source who tipped us? They're credible. And before you went into the rest stop, you had a quick exchange with someone in a car. That gives me reasonable grounds. So, hands on the hood."

The man muttered something under his breath as the officer began the pat-down. Abby felt her jaw tighten and she shivered in her lightweight cardigan as she buckled Carson into his car seat. She'd been right. The erratic movements, the bloodshot eyes—it had all lined up. Her radar was still tuned, sharp as ever.

And the local police were on it. She felt safer already.

After she ensured Carson's beloved teddy was snuggled in his arms, she started the portable DVD player strapped to the chair back in front of him. The screen lit up, and the theme song of Carson's favorite show rang out. Carson's head tipped to the side, and his cheek rested on the stuffed animal like a pillow. He'd be out in no time.

Abby merged back onto the highway and turned on her wipers. Traffic was light, but the wind howled, flattening thick rain hit her windshield. She fired up the narrated novel that had kept her entertained for the last four hours. Soon they passed the sign welcoming them to Southern Ontario's Green Belt. Chenaniah River wasn't much further.

Carson finally lost the battle with exhaustion. Cookie crumbs covered his chest, and bits of chocolate stuck to the corners of his mouth from the snacks she'd left within his reach.

Abby turned off the main highway and followed the SUV's built-in navigation system down a quiet country road. She hadn't planned to drive to her new job in the middle of the night, but when Austin and Sandy suddenly fell ill with flu-like symptoms, Abby cut their visit short. She hadn't wanted to catch whatever ailed her friends and potentially pass it to her new employer, William, or William's grandfather, her new client. Besides, William had left a key to the cottage under the mat so she could arrive anytime.

The rhythmic swish of the wiper blades and the ping of raindrops on the vehicle's body were strangely satisfying. The road dipped and rose, winding her deeper and deeper into wine country. From what she could see, the green belt lived up to its name. She crested the top of a hill and slammed her brakes at a sudden curve in the road.

Her tires clipped the graveled shoulder. Cranking the steering wheel hard to the left, her headlights raked across the horizon. Her stomach dropped at the sight of a burgeoning creek. She jerked to a stop, her pulse rioting. Tightening her grip on the steering wheel, she forced herself to take a deep breath.

If we had gone into the creek...

She glanced at Carson—still asleep—and swallowed hard. William Roth wasn't expecting them until tomorrow. No one would have even started looking for them until then.

Just breathe.

We're fine.

She straightened her cramping fingers. *We're fine,* she repeated to herself. She just needed her body to catch up with her mind. Another fifteen minutes, and they'd be in the picturesque town they'd be calling home.

A blue road sign for Hidden Valley Fruit Farm came into view. Abby rolled her shoulders, trying to release the tension in her muscles. They were almost there.

A final GPS prompt directed her down a private dirt road. A set of headlights glowed behind her, and her insides quivered. She'd give anything to turn off her internal radar. But her memories of time patrolling the streets with Austin were never far away. They edged into the new life she'd built with Carson, making her suspicious and jaded about things most people wouldn't notice, like a fellow traveler daring to drive on the same road as her.

The headlights cut out.

See. Just someone coming home after a night shift. She bit the inside of her cheek. The rain-streaked rear window blurred her sightline. She squinted, but it didn't help. All she could make out were the swaying tops of the trees that fenced the property. This was ridiculous. She likely had neighbors also renting from the prosperous fruit farmer, and most orchards employed migrant workers. The roar in her ears lessened. There was a time that she would have run toward danger and not away, but that was before Carson.

As the numbers on the dash clock flicked to 2:00 am, she parked in front of the cottage nearest to the right side of the main house and cut the engine. Carson slept. It would only take a few seconds to haul their two suitcases inside. Mr. Roth had promised the fully stocked cottage would have everything they needed to settle in initially. He even had his housekeeper make up the beds for them.

Holding her cardigan over her head to protect herself from the rain, she dashed to the porch. The motion-sensor lights activated. She palmed the promised key from underneath the welcome mat and, glancing back at Carson, breathed easier.

She'd cracked his door, so the car's interior light illuminated his face. Sliding the key into the lock, she unbolted it. She'd prop the door open, haul their bags from the trunk, then scoop up Carson and tuck him into bed.

A twig snapped nearby. Her chest tightened as she strained to sense the direction the sound came from. Was it the wind rustling the branches? The swoosh of fabric? A not-so-good Samaritan? Her heart raced. She didn't need to read crime novels or watch TV to imagine all the ways 2:00 am alone in the orchard could go wrong.

She shook her head. She was dehydrated, that was all. She should have had water not coffee. It was Post-Policing-Stress-Disorder. It wasn't an actual disorder, but it was the closest label she could come up with for how she felt. Always on high alert. Always waiting for the bullet to slam into her back. But there was no reason to be afraid anymore.

Until a hand grabbed her upper arm and jerked her down the porch stairs.

WILLIAM SHOT UPRIGHT IN BED. Gramps? Had he wandered out of his room again? A wet nose nudged his arm, and William threw off the bedcovers. He stuffed his feet into the slippers he kept by the bedside, tugged on a bathrobe, and belted it at the waist. Dreyfuss usually slept in the mudroom. Something had stirred the German Shepherd—something out of the ordinary.

William's watch screen lit up with his movements. 2:00 am. Gramps should be sound asleep.

Dreyfuss whined.

It could be Ella. But Rose, the nanny, usually got to his daughter before her cries could wake him.

A cut-short scream jolted William fully awake. He bolted to the window and, pulling back the curtain, squinted out the rain-splattered glass. The yard was too dark to make out much of anything, which meant no one had triggered the motion sensor lights. Must've been a fox. They mimicked human sounds of distress, and the peach orchard had seen plenty of those over the years.

Never in a million years would William have thought a country orchard could make his grandparents independently wealthy, but Gramps and Grams had bought the farm long before Chenaniah River had morphed into a tourist destination. Nor would William have guessed a few years of bad financial decisions could nearly bankrupt them. But both were true.

William moved to the window on the other wall. If he were in the master suite, he'd have a clear view of the driveway, but he'd insisted that Gramps keep it, since the ensuite bath and extra space made it easier for the elderly man to get around. From this spot, he could see the row of cabins housing their seasonal workers, but all was quiet. A muffled sound drew his gaze right. Under the glow of his rental's porch light, two figures tussled.

William launched himself down the stairs, commanding Dreyfuss to follow. Gramps loved his companion dog, but right now, William loved that the German Shepherd had been bred to be protective.

Dreyfuss kept pace as they cleared the porch. William didn't give the command for the dog to run ahead. He didn't want to risk Dreyfuss mistaking a victim for an attacker.

The smaller figure charged the larger one, taking him down. Their legs and arms tangled before she—at least he thought it was a she—rebounded to her feet.

William hurdled the planter at the end of the path and skidded in the mud. His chest burned. One hand slapped the wet ground, and he regained his balance. The late spring air set his lungs on fire with an urgency the rain couldn't quench.

The woman's wet hair fanned out as she spun.

Almost there.

She hoofed her attacker in the gut. The man *oomphed* and stumbled backward. He fumbled with the open car door.

"Hey," William shouted, scrambling the final few yards.

The woman rammed the heel of her hand up into the man's chin. It connected with a sickening crack.

William skidded to a stop, restraining Dreyfuss with a hold on his collar. This woman had moves.

Her assailant fell backward, vulgarities spewing from his mouth. His gaze landed on Dreyfuss, who'd fixed on the man like a missile locked on its target. He flipped onto his front, scrambled to his feet, and darted into the shadowy tree line.

William released the dog's collar. "Get him, Dreyfuss."

The dog shot past the startled woman like a bullet.

"Are you okay?"

She spun, fists clenched, and swung.

William dodged the punch and held out his hands, edging away from her and away from the still-sleeping child illuminated in the backseat of her vehicle. "I'm just trying to help." He wished he had grabbed his phone on his way out of the house. They needed to get inside and call the cops.

She bolted into the void between him and the yawning vehicle door and dipped her head inside. The interior light lit her face as her chest pitched with gulps. She pulled out a sleepy child, but her frame stayed rigid. Rain streamed down her face. She didn't wipe it. Instead, she mirrored his movements, blocking the child with her body.

A light flickered across the property inside one of the cabins. His orchard manager, Jethro, would be over soon to see about the disturbance. Dreyfuss yipped somewhere in the trees.

The light did not distract the feisty mama bear. She kept her gaze on him, and his heart did a funny thump. "Miss Sinclair?" They didn't know each other beyond the brief interview they'd conducted over a video call. "I didn't expect you until tomorrow."

Her posture relaxed when he moved into the arc of the porch light so she could see his face. "I'm William Roth."

An engine revved in the distance, muffling Dreyfuss's barking. She stiffened again.

"Mommy?"

The tiny voice made William's heart lurch. Mamma's cub awakened.

The hard lines on her face softened, and she brushed her son's hair off his face. Then, with the child's weight supported on her hip, she thrust out her hand toward William, shifting gears with impressive ease. "Abigail Sinclair. Abby. It's nice to meet you."

He had to give her credit. The girl had spunk. She transitioned as if nothing had happened. No, that wasn't quite right. Her chest still heaved, and her eyes were still large. She wasn't as okay as she pretended to be. Her control was a facade.

He wrapped her smaller hand in his larger one, his rough

skin sanding her smoother flesh. After a millisecond, she retracted her hand.

The key to the cottage stuck out from where someone had stabbed it into the lock. He cleared the porch steps two at a time and opened the door. A quick glance confirmed everything appeared as it should be. Everything but her.

"Do you need to sit down?"

She hovered in the doorway, half on the covered porch and half inside the cottage, only looking away from him when Dreyfuss bounded up the stairs and sat at her heel. The dog dropped a scrap of fabric at her feet and cocked his head to the side.

When William bent to retrieve the material, she jumped. But she had the grace to look embarrassed at her unease. Her gaze flicked to her son, who appeared more curious about the dog than afraid. Dreyfuss shook, and the motion showered them in a spray of water.

Giggling, the boy rested his head against his mother's shoulder.

"Are you okay?" William didn't see blood, and she didn't seem to be overcompensating for an injury, but she hadn't spoken since introducing herself. Was she in shock? Her fair skin glowed under a flush of color, looking almost as soft as her child's. Dark eyes widened under a slash of red hair. A few more pounds could have softened her sharp cheekbones and angled jaw.

"Yes, thank you." The roughness of her voice surprised him. This was no damsel in distress.

"You're definitely better than the other guy, judging from what I saw as I ran over here." His body temp instantly skyrocketed over what almost happened, but she stood stone-still, in complete control.

She chuckled, and the softness of it lobbed another surprise his way. Her ability to laugh in the aftermath of an attack spiked his curiosity. Abigail Sinclair was more than he'd expected.

"You can come into the main house with me. I need to check on Gramps. After, we can call the police."

She flipped her attention to where the shadows blurred together. Was she wondering if her attacker would circle back? Would this incident change her mind about taking the position? Would he have to restart his search for a personal support worker from scratch?

Tiny creases at the corners of her mouth deepened as she tightened her lips. She shifted her son to her other hip. Was she recalling their interview? Before accepting the position that he'd outlined in great detail, she'd asked one question. Was Chenaniah River safe? He'd assured her it was.

"I can make up a guest room for you and Carson. You can share a room in the main house."

Her expression remained unreadable, chin lifting just slightly. The kind of look that said she wasn't used to leaning on anyone.

William pressed on. "I'd feel better, considering all that happened, if you'd at least wait for the police at the main house." He didn't add *where I know you're safe.*

She hesitated, and for a second, he thought she'd refuse. Then her shoulders eased, almost reluctantly.

She gave a short nod. "For tonight."

"Everything okay here, William?"

Abby spun, not having heard Jethro approach from behind. Her arms tightened around Carson.

"Yes, thanks, Jethro." William gestured to Abby. "This is

Abigail Sinclair. She's going to be taking care of Gramps. Abby, this is Jethro. He manages the orchard."

Abby accepted Jethro's extended hand, eyeing him up and down.

"Someone attacked Abby. We're going to the main house and calling the police."

Jethro's eyes widened. He was probably recalling the other odd happenings, and wondering, like William, if they were connected. "Can I do anything?"

"Maybe let the workers know the police might knock on their doors to ask if they'd heard anything."

Jethro nodded. "I can do that."

"We give our workers the option to live on the farm in a stretch of cabins along the west side of the property," William explained to Abby. "Several of them do. You can't see the cabins in the dark, but tomorrow you'll be able to."

"Nice to meet you, Abigail," Jethro said.

"Abby," she corrected.

"Abby." Jethro tipped an imaginary hat to her, and returned to his cabin, the darkness quickly absorbing him.

William couldn't walk to the main house empty-handed, and there was no way Abby would release her hold on Carson. "Can I get your bags from the trunk?"

She nodded again.

The rain had faded to a drizzle. He jogged to the vehicle while she released the trunk using the remote. He pulled out two suitcases. "Only two?"

Her cheeks flushed. "Someone will deliver the rest later."

Dreyfuss bounded between them, looking more like a family pet than a guard dog. His wet nose pushed playfully against Carson's foot, and the boy nuzzled into his mother's shoulder. But not before another giggle slipped out.

"To the house," William directed the dog.

Dreyfuss obediently trotted ahead of them.

"Oh, I forgot." Abby dashed to the SUV and reached into the backseat. She pulled out a stuffed bear. Carson snatched it and burrowed his face in the fur. She smiled sheepishly. "Carson won't sleep without him."

"I totally understand. Ella, my five-year-old daughter, has a favorite stuffed dog. It sleeps at the foot of her bed and spans the width of a twin mattress." The stuffed monstrosity was their compromise when he wouldn't allow Dreyfuss to sleep in her room.

They walked in companionable silence, listening to the squishing of their shoes on the soft earth. He motioned for Abby to enter the house first and plopped her bags onto the floor just inside the front door. Dreyfuss headed for his water bowl. His slurping carried over from the mudroom, where he also had a large pillow for a bed.

"Willy?" a feeble voice called from the second floor.

"I'll be up in a minute, Gramps."

William pointed to the couch and motioned to Abby that she could lay Carson there, who'd fallen back asleep. "I'll grab some towels and call the police."

Gramps appeared on the middle landing of the staircase and teetered on the edge of the next step. He didn't have his walker or his cane.

"Gramps, I said I'd be right up. I just have to make a quick call."

Gramps's bony fingers gripped the railing while he rubbed the palm of his other hand against his chest in small circles. "What's all the ruckus?"

"You probably heard me outside with Abigail. She arrived a bit earlier than expected and ran into a bit of trouble. I'm calling the police." William's chest ached at the man's frailty. How many times would they have this same conversation? Gramps wasn't as strong as he used to be. He wasn't supposed to try to manage the stairs alone.

William kept his voice gentle. It didn't matter how often he repeated these words; he'd never be harsh with his grandfather. He was the father William never had. "What are you doing out of bed? You know I'll come to you."

"I called and called. No one came."

William's throat thickened. He had one job. Take care of Grandpa and Ella. And he couldn't even do that right.

Gramps looked at Abigail, who watched them from the sofa. "You trust the cops?"

She smiled. "I do."

"They never did anything about the home," Gramps said.

William sighed. "Gramps—"

"There's still rot in the wood. You watch yourself," Gramps said. When his gaze landed on Carson, it softened considerably. "And who's the little guy?"

"That's Abby's son, Carson. They'll be staying in the cottage."

Assuming she didn't quit after tonight.

"Carson," Gramps repeated.

William would probably have to tell him Carson's name several times before he remembered—if he remembered. Hopefully, Abby was ready for the difficulties of dementia.

"What's his name?" Gramps asked.

William missed the man Gramps once was. "Carson."

Gramps opened his mouth as if he was about to repeat the name and collapsed.

CHAPTER
TWO

Abby sprang to her feet. William had caught his grandfather, who'd slumped and compressed. He slid down the corner where the two walls of the landing met. But supporting the dead weight of a grown man was a two-person job. Abby ducked under Robert Roth's left side and shifted some of the load to her.

"Let's get him to the couch."

The sitting room had two matching sofas that faced each other. Abby steered them toward the empty one. Carson slept on one, and William's pale grandfather now stretched out on the other. They'd hardly gotten him down when he started to rouse and slap away their help.

Robert rubbed his face. "What happened?"

"Mr. Roth, are you okay?" Abby leaned over him. His pupils were even. The cloudiness was lifting, and color was returning to his cheeks. Robert struggled to push himself up on his elbows.

Abby placed a gentle hand on his shoulder. "Not so fast. We're not sure what happened."

"Should we call an ambulance?" The tendons in William's neck bulged.

"No, thank you," Mr. Roth said more forcefully this time. "If I'm gonna die, I'll do it right here in my own house."

Abby's mouth twitched. The man had spunk, and the fact it had returned indicated whatever took him down had passed.

William paced. "This is not up for discussion, Gramps. I'm calling the ambulance."

Robert tensed under Abby's fingers, which she had slid down to his wrist to secretly count his pulse.

"Just call Dr. Pike," Robert said. "He said I could call anytime."

William continued to pace. The belt on his robe loosened with each step and revealed hints of his rain-soaked t-shirt and blue plaid pajama bottoms, also wet from their adventure outdoors. A chunk of his dark hair fell forward over one eye, and the bristles of a five o'clock shadow softened his jawline. She shifted her focus back to Robert.

"Who's Dr. Pike?"

"Dr. Pike is a family friend," William said to Abby before looking back at Robert. "And he will not want to come out here in the middle of the night."

Robert scowled and mumbled some more under his breath. His mannerisms and sour face reminded Abby of Carson when he pouted.

William's refusal to defer to his grandfather's wishes riled the man, which could raise his blood pressure and cause another incident. "Calling a friend sounds like a good compromise to me," Abby said. "He could advise you on whether a trip to the hospital is necessary."

William sighed and stabbed a few buttons on his phone and strode into the other room. Abby could hear murmurs of his conversation but no words. She gave Mr. Roth Sr. her full attention. "Do you know what happened?"

"I got lightheaded, that's all." His eyes followed William, and then he lowered his voice. "They're trying to kill me, you know."

Her heart quickened, but not with concern. William had hinted at Robert's eccentricity. Robert had a list of wild theories a mile long that contained details about the invisible people trying to take him out. William said he'd always been a bit of a conspiracy nut, but it was benign stuff. Like the royal plot to kill Princess Di or the extraterrestrials the American government hid in Area 52. But over the last year, the theories had dialed up. It's partly what convinced William to seek private care. William said he needed someone with an unbiased opinion to weigh in on whether it might be time to move his grandfather back into a long-term care home. William's Uncle Joe was still angry William moved Gramps home. He thought his dad needed more care, but William wanted to give Robert as much time as possible in the home he'd loved for decades.

"Who's trying to kill you?" Abby didn't crack a smile. She didn't dare, but she also knew better than to dismiss Robert entirely. If she'd learned anything working with the elderly, it was that people didn't give them enough credit.

"The government. I know too much."

She slipped a cushion under Robert's head. His eyes closed, and his hollow cheeks sagged, exhaustion carved into every wrinkle.

She stroked his thin gray hair, moving her fingers slowly, massaging a little as she did for Carson when he was too worked up to fall asleep. "I won't let anyone hurt you."

Gramps snorted. He actually snorted as if that was the funniest thing he'd heard all day. His eyes opened a slit. Just enough to read her expression. "What's a pipsqueak like you going to do if trouble breaks out?"

"She'll take him down." William answered for her, pocketing his phone as he rejoined them. He handed her a towel the same color as the one he'd slung around his neck. He'd changed into sweatpants and a sweatshirt. "Just like she did with that prowler outside."

Abby busied herself toweling her hair. The admiration in William's voice buoyed her confidence.

"There was a prowler outside?" Gramps pushed himself upright.

"Whoever was there is gone now," Abby assured him. At least he better be. Abby looked pointedly at William. "Your grandfather thinks someone is trying to hurt him."

The doorbell rang, and William moved to answer it.

Robert's panicked gaze shot to the foyer.

"A villain doesn't ring the doorbell." Abby assured him. Robert's posture relaxed a smidge. Abby might have even caught the start of a smile.

Abby stood as Dr. Pike followed William into the room and accepted his offered handshake as William introduced them.

"Welcome to Chenaniah River." The doctor's warm greeting did little to heat the cold that gripped the back of her neck and refused to release. Her tussle outside hadn't fully registered in her mind yet. Her body was still reacting. But that wasn't the doctor's fault.

"Thank you. I'll give you some privacy."

Her steps hitched by Carson, who was still asleep.

"He'll be okay," Dr. Pike assured her. "I'll call you if he stirs."

William motioned for Abby to follow him.

"You could have stayed with your grandfather." Stress tightened like a winch in her midsection.

"I wanted a minute with you." William stuffed both hands into the pockets of his joggers. "Gramps has been telling tales for as long as I can remember, but he's never said someone was trying to kill him."

She reached out, only giving William's upper arm a brief squeeze before letting go. He was more on edge than she was. She forced herself to let go and gripped the towel slung around her neck to give her hands something to do. "I've seen this before. Elderly patients can easily become confused, especially if their blood sugar drops or medications get mixed up."

"But on the heels of what happened to you..."

He didn't need to finish his sentence for Abby to follow his thoughts. Were the two events connected?

She glanced back into the living room. The doctor had pulled a chair close to the sofa. He and Robert spoke too softly for them to hear, but she imagined Robert telling the doc not to worry his grandson. Her heart panged. What would it be like to have generational love like that? Abby had been an only child, and she lost her parents right before she turned eighteen. Carson would never know bedtime traditions with his grandparents.

William's breath caught with a crackle. "Gramps isn't crazy. Sure, he put his money into organizations that explored extraterrestrial life and secret governments, but he's also poured thousands into global healthcare through humanitarian foundations."

She frowned. "Who said he was crazy?"

"He's a contradiction," William continued. "A man who likes to play devil's advocate. But now that he needs care, he's refusing it. He's sent more caregivers running by being obstinate, and I can't take care of him alone." William chuckled. It was warm and deep, and she liked how it conveyed his love for his grandfather.

"I don't scare easily." She looked him dead in the eyes and held it until he nodded.

A porch board groaned on the other side of the front door, and the outside motion lights triggered. William moved toward the sound. "That should be the police. I called them after phoning Dr. Pike."

The doorknob slowly twisted, and instinct kicked in. Abby yanked William back before he could swing the door open. "They'd knock," she whispered. "They wouldn't let themselves in." Her breathing echoed in her ears.

The doorknob rattled. Louder this time.

Abby pounded on the door with the side of her fist. "The police are on their way."

A shuffle. A scuffing sound of feet on boards. Then, the porch lights backlit a figure in front of the window, casting a shadow against the pulled drapes. The window rattled.

Someone was trying to get in!

William called Dreyfuss. The window rattled louder, and a growl rumbled from deep in the animal's chest.

"If you don't leave right now," William announced, "I'll let the dog out."

The rattling stopped, and the shadow retreated, growing smaller and smaller.

22

Headlights came up the driveway, and the figure scurried away. Abby pulled the corner of the curtain back to peek outside and sagged as a police cruiser parked. "The police are here." *Finally.*

They were coming up to 3:00 am, but the two police officers that joined them seemed just as fresh as she would have expected mid-day. They introduced themselves as Detective Andy Reuben and Officer Gavin Thorn. Cutbacks meant more police rode solo, so the fact two stood on the doorstep told Abby one was probably a rookie, likely Gavin because of his age. She addressed the older man, who seemed to be friends with William, and provided a quick summary of the night and disclosed her history on the police force. While the officers checked the property, Abby paced in the foyer. She needed to stay near Carson but wanted to know the details of the investigation. Finally, they confirmed their unwanted guest had appeared to have moved on.

"Excuse me." Dr. Pike saved her from follow-up questions. "I'd like to take Robert to the hospital. Everything seems fine, but he hasn't passed out before. I'd rather be safe than sorry. I already called an ambulance. They'll arrive without sirens since it is not an emergency. I also called Joe. He'll meet us at the hospital."

William frowned.

Abby didn't know who Joe was, but William was clearly annoyed the doctor had involved him.

"I asked Robert first," the doctor said. "Is there a reason you don't want your uncle involved?"

"It's fine." William hurried to Gramps. He bent to whisper a few words in his ear and then turned to her. "I'll wake Rose. I told you about her. She helps me with Ella. Carson can sleep in the room next to Ella's while we accompany the officers to the cottage and then go to the hospital. There's no rush for us to get there since my Uncle Joe is going."

The way William's nose curled at the mention of Uncle Joe spiked her curiosity. William called Dreyfuss to his side.

Scooping up Carson, Abby followed William down the hallway. Carson's head rolled against her. She moved him to the spare bedroom William pointed out, and Rose opened the joining door to Ella's room, where William's daughter slept peacefully.

The rumpled grandmotherly woman claimed the rocking chair and picked up a Bible from a basket on the floor. "William told me about your unfortunate welcome. I will stay awake until you get back. I'll pray."

"Thank you." The words stuck in her throat. She took this job so she could keep Carson safe, but nothing about tonight had felt safe. Could she leave Carson with this woman?

"Dreyfuss, guard," William commanded.

The dog straightened, and he sat at attention at Rose's heel.

As Abby tucked the blankets around Carson, the rounds of his cheeks flushed pink, and his red lips puckered. He gripped Bear-be and snuggled in.

Abby pressed her lips to his forehead. *What have I gotten us into?*

WILLIAM STARED across the property at the lit-up cottage. Any evidence left behind by their visitor had likely been washed away by the steady rain, so there wasn't any hurry to join the officers who were already processing the scene.

Abby looked impossibly fresh for 3:00 am. She'd pulled

her hair into a wet knot at the nape of her neck and changed into leggings and a lightweight sweatshirt with some sort of police logo on the front. When they stepped off the bottom porch step, they triggered the motion sensors.

The outlines of Andy and Gavin waiting for them at the cottage grew clearer with each step. William attended church with Andy. He was a good guy. He'd get to the bottom of this. His friend rocked from his heels to the balls of his feet. Gavin watched Andy and mimicked his movements and mannerisms.

"The inside is trashed." Andy started speaking the second William's foot hit the bottom step. "Did you leave it unlocked?"

William hesitated. He remembered unlocking the cottage. He didn't remember locking it again. "I don't recall."

Gavin had his notebook out and was taking notes. "Do you know why someone would be sneaking around the property?"

"No."

Abby's demeanor shifted. It was subtle, like the alter-ego in a comic book removing his glasses and morphing into a hero. She changed from a personal support worker to a cop. "Is the scene secured? Can we go inside?"

Andy nodded permission. "It would help to know if anything is missing."

Nausea weakened William's knees as he nudged the front door the rest of the way open. But the first emotion to follow the nausea wasn't fear. It was thankfulness that Abby and Carson had come to the main house and were protected from this.

While he wandered through the small space, checking for the television and other minor electronics they kept in the cottage for guests, disbelief hardened his gut. Chenaniah River wasn't a perfect town despite how tourism promoted it. William would even say the crime rate was low. Incidents were mostly petty theft, which this couldn't be since the television—the most valuable item in the cottage—was still here. And what were the odds of a random Break and Enter occurring right after someone attacked Abby?

Even the sofa cushions were shredded. The sight of the overturned furniture and emptied cupboards crushed him. The refrigerator door hung open, and the meals Rose had prepared as a welcome had all been destroyed. It didn't feel random. It felt personal.

"Any guess what they were looking for?" Abby's question landed gently. She briefly touched his arm to get his attention, and his chest hummed at the contact.

This would be the final nail in the coffin. There was no way Abby would stay after this, and he couldn't blame her. His head felt like a bruised peach after a hailstorm. "Not a clue."

"Has anything unusual happened lately?" She moved papers strewn across the table using the eraser on a pencil. She skimmed the pages and then moved to the mess on the kitchen counter. The way she avoided using her hands reminded him of the cops he saw on television.

Unusual events? That was a great question. How about accounting that wouldn't balance? An elderly man convinced someone was trying to kill him? A daughter that still had nightmares? But none of those things were unusual. They'd become so normal they hardly registered anymore. "Someone damaged several fruit trees, and Gramps has been ill."

She paused. "How ill?"

"Not enough to call the doctor, but enough to keep Gramps within a fifty-foot radius of the restroom. We've had a couple of hang-up calls in the middle of the night. Pranks." At least, he thought they were pranks.

"How do you know the tree damage wasn't a natural occurrence?" Andy's question jolted him. William had forgotten that Andy and Gavin were there.

"Jethro told me that someone slashed the trunks of some trees and introduced Peach Tree Borers. Thankfully, he had used a preventative spray that took out the larvae, and we could save the infected trees. The borers could have been natural, but they gained access to the trunk through the slashes, which were not natural."

Gavin kept making notes in his book. "What cabin does Jethro live in?"

"Number seven."

"Did you see this?" Abby addressed Andy, but William moved closer to look.

Andy snapped on latex gloves and picked up a piece of paper that had something scribbled on it. Andy held up the paper so William could read it.

I'm just getting started.

"What's just starting? Is it a threat? An innocent note that reads ominously because of this?" Abby gestured to the destroyed room. She drilled her gaze so deeply into William he was sure she could see his soul.

"I don't know. In your interview, you said you were a whistleblower. Could this be backlash?"

Abby hesitated long enough that Andy frowned at her. "I'll need the details about that."

"It's nothing," Abby said with a wave of her hand. But red spread across the back of her neck. "A staff member from the nursing home I worked at was pocketing pain medication to support her addiction. I outed her."

Andy kept his gaze fixed on Abby. "Do you think she could have followed you here?"

"The person who attacked me was male."

"She might have a boyfriend," Gavin said.

"We're going to need her name and contact information so we can follow up," Andy said before shifting to William. "When was the last time you had a guest in here?"

William scratched the back of his neck. "My cousin from out East came for a bit last summer, but Rose was in here last week to get the place ready for Abigail. Our seasonal workers started months ago, but they stay in the cabins."

If Gramps were here, he'd spin some tale about the government, organized crime, or even alien life playing a role in tonight's adventures. There would be some crazy reason for everything that went down tonight. William could only hope that Gramps wouldn't fixate on Abigail as the enemy, but would see her as an ally. Otherwise, the feisty PSW would be done before she started.

Andy closed his notebook and slipped it into his pocket. "I'd like to bring out forensics to examine the scene so we know what we're dealing with. Do you have another place Ms. Sinclair can stay until we are finished?"

"She can stay in the main house, if that's okay with her." William looked at Abby for her agreement. He got the feeling she wasn't the type of woman to take orders.

"That sounds good. Thank you."

Relief loosened his coiled muscles. "If you don't need us for anything else, we need to get to the hospital."

"You go ahead. We'll be here a while."

Abby dug into her purse and retrieved her remote. She

clicked a button, and her SUV's headlights flashed. "I can drive."

Abby pulled onto the main road, and William scrambled for something to say and came up blank. This was hardly the welcome he'd hoped to give his grandfather's new worker. He had to say something—anything—before she gave her notice, packed up her son, and left.

But Abby broke the silence first. "How long have you had Dreyfuss?"

Dreyfuss. A safe topic. "About four years. We got him from a local guy, Frankie Berns. He rescues and trains dogs. He's good company for Gramps, and Ella always wanted a dog. Especially after her mom got sick."

"I'm sorry you lost your wife." Usually, when people offered condolences, William bristled. Their expressions changed, and they pulled back. Grief frightened off all but the closest of friends. But as Abby held his eyes, hers filled with understanding, and he knew. Abigail Sinclair had once lost someone important to her.

"Thank you." His swollen throat made it hard to push out the words. Grief never got easier. He'd known early on that his wife wouldn't make it. He'd known almost from the beginning. By the time she died, William had lived a million contradictions, wanting it to be over while he prayed for one more day. He couldn't stand watching her suffer. He prayed it would end, even if it meant losing her, but then they desperately tried everything to save her. What kind of husband was so double-minded? Especially when Ella begged God every night to save her mother.

"Something's wrong." Abby frowned. The vehicle sputtered, chugged, and powered down. She steered to the side of the road. "I don't like this."

The beams from the headlights only reached a few feet. After that, darkness.

Abby flicked the key a few times. Nothing. "It's like we ran out of gas, but the gauge says the tank is half full."

"Pop the hood. I'll take a look." He hopped out of the vehicle, trying not to think about what could be hiding in the bushes. He lifted the hood and propped it open with the metal arm.

Abby opened the driver's door so they could talk. "You know cars?"

"More than most." There was a time he thought he'd be a mechanic. He even worked in a garage for a bit before changing courses and going into business, but she didn't need to know all that. He studied the engine under his phone light. "Nothing looks out of place."

The branches in the ditch rustled, stealing his retort. He thought of the note.

I'm just getting started.

Stranded like this, they were vulnerable. His pulse throbbed in his neck, and the pressure in his skull increased. He struggled to bring his mind under control. He didn't do this. He didn't jump to the worst case scenario. The note was innocent. The noise was the wind moving the trees or wildlife.

"Are you okay?"

It was just the wind. His scalp prickled. "I'm going to slide under the back and see if the fuel line is good." The SUV sat high enough that he should be able to see the lines without jacking up the backend. The natural noises of the countryside bellowed through his senses. Did she hear it too?

Damp earth seeped through the back of his sweatshirt. Using his light, he followed the gas line all the way to a clamp near the fuel tank. Someone had pinched off her gas supply. It wouldn't take more than ten seconds for a guy who knew cars to do this, and the location of the clamp indicated the perpetrator knew what he was doing. Had he clamped closer to the engine, she would have only been able to drive about fifteen seconds. Hardly long enough to get off his property. But clamping here gave her a minute, maybe more. Just enough to isolate her. William removed the device and hurried back into the vehicle, immediately locking the doors. "Try it now."

After a few seconds, the engine fired up. Abby eyed the clamp in his hands and scowled. "Do we need the police again?"

"I'm afraid we do." William's head started to throb. If the plan had been to isolate them, why hadn't someone made a move while they were on the side of the road? Unless the perpetrator was waiting to get Abby alone.

CHAPTER
THREE

Abby spent much of the night vacillating between staying in Chenaniah River and leaving. Leaving meant safety, but it also meant starting over again. And she was out of options.

She rested a hand on Carson's blond head. "I need you to be on your best behavior. Mr. Roth is not feeling well."

Carson skipped alongside her. His thumbs looped through the straps of his teddy bear backpack, and the bear's head bobbed with each step. He lifted his chin to look up at her, and he unhooked one thumb and trailed his fingers along the hospital corridor. "Rose said I can call him Gramps."

"Did she?" Abby clenched at the familiar term. She didn't plan to invest emotionally in the Roth family any more than she usually invested, but she could hardly tell a four-year-old to keep his distance. It wasn't Carson's fault that she wasn't one hundred percent sure she wanted to stay in Chenaniah River after their welcome. Especially since staying meant taking up temporary residence in the main house with William's family.

It wouldn't be good for Carson to develop an attachment to the Roths. Calling the older man Gramps was the start of a bond that would eventually break. If Robert's dementia sparked his paranoia, it was likely their partnership wouldn't work out. Because if that happened, he'd need more care than she could offer. Even the best-case scenario was grim. If it worked out, Robert's health was on a downward trend. They'd get two, maybe three years tops from this placement. Carson was too young to understand that his welcome into the family was conditional on her employment.

But she didn't say any of that. The other half of her brain was busy arguing that this invitation was a blessing. Male role models would be good for Carson, however long the Lord saw fit to grant them. Her double-mindedness befuddled her. She usually had a clearer head regarding her son and appropriate boundaries, but her heart ached for all she could never provide him, and that aching fuzzed the lines.

Carson longed for a father figure. Austin was a surrogate grandpa, but they didn't live close enough to him and Sandy for them to really shape Carson. Whoever Carson spent the most time with would have the loudest voice. So she'd looked into William before she accepted the job. He was a generous community supporter, active in his church, and had no criminal record. She wouldn't take her son just anywhere.

"Gramps," Abby tried it out, "is coming home today. We get to bring him home."

"We bring Gramps home," Carson repeated in his sing-song voice. The bear's head kept bobbing with each step.

Home. The word curled in her midsection like a snake

preparing to strike. Despite living in lots of places, none of them had been home. She wouldn't let them. Not since the fire.

She chewed on the inside of her cheek. If William ran a background check on her, would it reveal how her parents died? She shoved the thought aside and rapped her knuckles on Robert's door as they entered. "Knock, knock."

William and Robert sat with a checkerboard between them. Abby and Carson had traveled here with William, who had insisted her SUV get a thorough once over from his mechanic before she drove it again. She and Carson had stopped at the gift shop in the hospital lobby to pick up a treat for Robert and to provide him and William a few minutes alone.

Robert completed a double jump and whooped. He thrust his fist into the air and made Carson giggle.

"How are you feeling today, Robert?"

"Call me Gramps. Robert's my dad." Robert didn't take his eyes off the playing board.

Her insides squished at the invitation.

"What do you think my next move should be, Carson?" William patted the chair beside him. "You just missed Uncle Joe," William said to her.

Carson climbed onto the vinyl seat and perched on his knees. With one hand on William's arm to steady himself, he leaned over and peered at the playing board with all the seriousness of a football player studying the plan for a Hail Mary play in the last few seconds of a game.

Carson didn't know how to play checkers. She'd never thought about teaching him. As William quietly explained the game, the snake inside coiled tighter. What else had she failed to teach her boy?

"William says you used to be a cop?" Robert eyed her with a clear and discerning gaze. That was the funny thing about dementia. Some moments were clear, and others were muddled.

"I was." She handed Robert the card Carson had picked out. "Do you need help from law enforcement?"

Gramps huffed. "Ain't no cop able to help me, not when they have access to my food. It's in the food."

"Gramps," William interrupted gently.

"Who has access to your food?" Abby spoke over William. She had completely understood the look William had given her, but ignored it. She wanted to hear Robert's theories from Robert's lips.

"The government." Robert's hand slapped the table. The checker pieces rattled and rolled a few inches. Carson jumped.

William steadied the table and repositioned the shifted playing discs while smiling reassuringly at Carson. "Don't get yourself riled, Gramps."

William might have addressed Robert, but he directed the correction at her.

"Why do you think the government would spike your food?" Abby ignored William again, noting the way his skin puckered between his eyes when he frowned.

"I gotta go potty." Carson jerked upright. He slid off the cushion and landed with a little foot dance.

"The restroom in this room is only for the patient." Abby held out a hand to Carson. "The public restrooms are down the hall. We'll be right back." She winked at Robert.

William followed her and Carson into the hallway. "I don't want you encouraging Gramps in his theories."

Abby scanned the signage and quickened her steps,

reaching the bathroom in record time. She pushed the bathroom door, but Carson stopped and tried to pull his hand free. "No."

She tightened her grip on him. "What do you mean, no?"

"I wanna go in the boys' room." Carson pointed at the adjacent door with the pictogram of a man on the front.

She pressed her lips together. From the corner of her eye, she could see William watching them. She didn't need Carson throwing a tantrum in front of her new boss. She stooped over and placed her hands on her knees. "I can't go in there. Mommy is a girl. I can only take you into the women's restroom."

"But I'm a boy." Carson's bottom lip protruded, and his tiny foot stamped. Even at four, he knew something was different about their family. Being a single mom slayed her at the oddest moments. Carson didn't have a man to do something as basic as taking him into the bathroom.

"Carson, if you need to go, we only have one option. This one." She pointed at the door. There was no way she was walking into the men's room, and the hospital didn't have a family restroom.

"I don't hafta go." The way he twisted his lower body undermined his confident statement. They were seconds away from a puddle forming under his feet.

"Can I help?" William laced his gentle offer with an amused smile. Not a mocking one, but the smile of a comrade. A man who knew what it was to battle a child's logic. "I've been on the other end of this argument. How about if I take Carson into the men's room, and the next time we're out, you can take Ella into the women's room?"

Abby bit her lower lip. William's intentions were probably pure. He totally got that this was not ideal. But she'd never let anyone else help Carson in this area.

Carson started to hop. "I gotta go now." He stretched the word *now* over four syllables.

She reached for his hand. "I'll take you."

Carson tucked his hands behind him. "I'm a boy."

"A boy about to pee his pants."

Carson's lip protruded further.

Abby sighed. It was let William take Carson or clean up a mess on the hospital floor. When Carson dug in like this, he would not back down. She briefly considered scooping him up and carrying him into the restroom, but the likely outcome was he'd lose bladder control in the struggle, and she'd need to change her clothes as much as he did.

"Can you manage everything yourself, Carson? Mr. Roth will not help you wipe." Heat filled her cheeks. She reminded herself that William had a daughter close to Carson's age. So, none of this would be new to him.

"I can do it." Carson pushed against the men's door. It hardly moved.

William put one hand on the door above Carson's. "Why don't you visit Gramps?" he said to her. "I'll text you if Carson needs you, and I'll let you know when it's safe to enter if any—ah—wiping needs to happen."

She appreciated how he tried to keep his expression neutral and not laugh at her son.

Hot pressure pushed against the back of her eyes. There was a reason that families had two parents. But she couldn't rewrite history. She couldn't make Carson's dad want to be part of their life any more than she could force God to answer her prayers.

"Okay."

William pushed the door open, and Carson hurried inside.

Lord, help Carson.

It automatically came out. Her muscle memory returned to the Lord because her parents had ingrained in her He was always there. He was the only One that would never leave her. She never doubted it until the fire. Because if it were true, it meant He was there the night her parents died. He was there and didn't stop it. She'd never known what to do about that, so she practiced a faith of contradictions. She called out to God, unconvinced that He'd intervene and help her. She taught Carson about God, unconvinced that He truly cared about them. She believed in God. She just wasn't sure she trusted Him anymore.

Abby stared at her silent phone. The time changed by one minute, and she stuffed her phone into her back pocket. She could linger here like a helicopter parent or see Robert and take advantage of a few minutes alone to ask the pertinent medical questions that William couldn't answer for her.

"Robert?" She tapped her knuckles on the door again, announcing her arrival.

Robert's soft snores exhaled in even beats.

She should let him rest. He probably didn't have a quiet night. Hospitals were difficult places to sleep.

As she turned to leave, a body lurched from behind the door. Abby reacted, but it wasn't quick enough. He got the drop on her. Hands shoved. A blur of blue. A whiff of sweat and metal. She landed on the bedside tray, which wheeled out from under her. Checkers scattered, pinging off the floor. The lunch tray clattered.

Robert gasped awake. His arms flailed for the panic button.

Abby's temple clipped the bed rail as she went down. A booted foot connected with her gut. She swung out and took out her attacker's legs. He hit the ground and cursed. It was enough for her to know he was male.

The room fuzzed around the edges.

He hoisted himself onto his hands and knees and scurried out the door.

Dizziness disoriented her.

More feet rushed in. Someone rolled her onto her back.

She pushed the hands away. "I'm fine. I'm fine."

Fingers pressed to her pulse. More bodies huddled around the bed. *Robert!*

She tried to sit up. Someone supported her. The bed, chair, and legs of the person in front of her swayed. She strained to see what was happening to Robert.

Was he okay? Hands hurried over the man. Blinking failed to clear her vision. Did the shock of the attack send him into cardiac arrest? Had the intruder given Gramps something before she arrived?

Her phone vibrated in her pocket.

Carson.

"I DON'T THINK your mom is coming, Champ. You're going to have to do the best you can." William encouraged Carson through the stall door. Abby hadn't responded to his text messages. His multiple text messages. His gut screamed something was off, but he had nothing solid to base the instinct on. He didn't really know Abby, but after her reluctance to let him help Carson, he'd expected a quick reply.

"All done." The toilet flushed.

William opened the door and led Carson to the sink.

"Now you have to wash your hands." Carson couldn't quite reach the faucet, so William looped his forearms under Carson's armpits and hoisted him a few inches off the floor. Carson finished up, and they exited the restroom.

As they neared Gramps's room, the air charged and intensified. Not a code-blue kind of rush, but the sound system repeated a code William didn't recognize. He picked up the pace.

A man powered toward them like a linebacker in a blue jersey. His chin tucked into his chest, and his body knocked Carson as they passed. "Watch out," he growled.

William tightened his grip on Carson's hand. "You okay?"

Carson nodded.

The closer they got to Gramps's room, the harder the ball in William's stomach clenched. This was ground zero.

"Where's Mommy?" There was the tiniest wobble to the question. Carson's head swiveled, taking in the chaos. The code repeated on the loudspeaker. Staff rushed around. Carson's lower lip trembled, and he clutched the strap of his knapsack.

"With Gramps. I'll get her. Stay right here at this door." William waited until Carson nodded before straightening to his full height. He briefly held his breath. He didn't know what he'd find in Gramps's room, but he knew whatever it was, it wasn't meant for Carson's eyes.

The machines connected to Gramps beeped. William might have thought he was sleeping if not for the several sets of hands moving over his body. A nurse barked commands. Gramps's chest rose and fell in a steady pattern.

A doctor crouched near the foot of the bed on the floor. The hem of his white coat dusted the vinyl flooring.

Abby! William's heart slammed against his ribs. The

beginnings of a bruise shadowed the right side of Abby's cheek.

A nurse jostled him as she brushed by. "Here's the cold pack."

The doctor activated it and pressed it against Abby's injury. "Can you tell me where you are?"

"Grand River Hospital."

"What day is it?"

"May 25th."

"How many fingers do you see?" He held up three fingers.

After Abby passed a few more tests, the doctor straightened. "I think you'll be okay. You'll have a shiner for a few days."

Abby looked up at the doctor and noticed William behind him. Her gaze sharpened. "Where's Carson?"

"What happened?"

They spoke at the same time.

"Carson's in the hall. I didn't want him to see if Gramps had—" His voice cracked.

Understanding filled her gaze. Still, it flicked anxiously to the doorway. Before she could even try, the doctor placed a hand on her shoulder and squeezed it. "You're not standing up just yet." He helped her to a chair instead.

Abby winced, but obeyed. "Someone knocked me from behind when I entered."

William used the wall to steady himself. Of all the things he could have imagined she'd say, that never made the list. Someone shoved a chair underneath him before he replaced Abby on the floor.

"Gramps?"

"He's fine." The nurse pressing buttons on the machine

attached to Gramps answered. "Whatever the person had planned, your friend's arrival stopped him."

Pressure built behind his eyes. She stopped him. *Stopped who?*

"Mommy?" the small voice interrupted. Right. Carson.

"I'll get him." William pushed off the chair.

"You'll be okay." He could hear the doctor assuring Abby. "Over-the-counter pain meds and ice should do the trick, but come back in if anything seems to worsen."

"Hey, buddy." William ruffled Carson's hair. "You did a good job staying put." Carson slipped his little hand into his. Something about his hold on Carson felt different from when Ella held his hand.

Carson's stride shortened with uncertainty. It would have been impossible for the child to miss that something important had happened here. His gaze bounced all over the room, wide and hesitant, until it latched onto his mother. He threw himself at her.

Abby winced as his body hit, but she wrapped her arms around him and pulled him close anyway. She pressed her face into his hair. Her eyes closed, and her lips moved.

William hoped she was thanking God. This could have gone wrong a million ways.

"Why do you have that?" Carson pointed at the cold pack still clutched in her hand.

"I banged my head."

Carson's fingers grazed her skin with the gentlest touch. "Owie?"

A ghost of a smile crossed her face. "Yes, it hurts. But it'll be better soon."

William frowned. Lingering behind her declaration had to be all sorts of doubts. She had hardly been in town for twenty-four hours, and she'd been attacked twice and her vehicle sabotaged. William might question *her* mental health if she didn't give him her notice today.

A shadow filled the doorway, and surprise colored Andy Reuben's face as he recognized Abby. "You again?"

She turned her weak smile his way. "I'd like to lodge a complaint against whoever runs your community's welcome program."

William's jaw slackened. How could she joke?

Andy eyed Gramps, who was now sedated. "Officer Gavin is speaking with the nurses, but can you tell me what you think happened here?"

The million-dollar question. William leaned in.

Abby adjusted Carson on her lap and dampened her lips. "I'm not sure. I entered the room. Gramps was asleep. At least, I think he was asleep." She pressed her fingertips to her forehead. Her hand trembled. "I was going to leave, let him rest, when someone shoved me from behind."

"Can you describe your attacker?"

"He was about your size. Unfortunately, I didn't get a good look at his face."

"Him? You're sure he was male?"

"Positive. I hit my head on the bed rail. I think that's what woke up Gramps. The table clattered noisily. The man kicked me."

"Kicked you?" Andy stopped writing on his notepad.

"Why wouldn't he just run?" William asked.

"I don't know, but it's curious." Andy's eyebrows pulled together as he made a few more notes in his notebook.

"I swept his legs out from under him, and when he went down, he cursed. Definitely a male voice."

Of course, she took him down. The image of her battling

her attacker at the farm resurfaced. Abby Sinclair was a force to be reckoned with.

"My head was foggy. I might have passed out for a few seconds. The next thing I knew, the nurses were here trying to rouse me."

"Do you think this is connected to what happened yesterday?" William asked. Needing something to do with his hands, William stuffed them into his pockets. His gaze drilled into Andy. He hated feeling so helpless.

Andy lifted a shoulder. "I don't have enough information to say, but I don't believe in coincidences."

"I'm sorry he got away." Abby's voice trailed off.

Andy's face tightened. "Sometimes they get away. You're still here, and that matters more. It wasn't your job to detain him. Your job was to survive."

Abby stared back at Andy for a long minute, her expression equally tight. Sensing the moment's seriousness in a way kids often could, Carson laid his head against her chest.

A silent communication passed between Andy and Abby. Something from officer to officer that William didn't understand.

Andy closed his notebook and tucked it back into his shirt pocket. He handed Abby his card for the second time in less than twenty-four hours. "Call me if you need me. Anything. Don't hesitate."

She took the card. She couldn't slip it into her pocket with Carson on her lap, so she just held it.

Andy stuck out his hand to William. "You know how to get ahold of me. Trust your gut. Something fishy is going on."

William shook Andy's hand, and Andy left.

Abby gently prodded the deepening blue mark on her face.

"Let's get you home." William held out his arms to Carson, and Abby handed him over. Her willingness to relinquish Carson said more about her condition than anything else. William stopped at the nurses' station for an update on their plan for Gramps. Considering what happened, Gramps needed to stay longer. They cautioned Abby not to drive, and she agreed, assuring the nurse William was driving her home. William balanced Carson on his hip and cupped Abby's elbow with his other hand. He helped her to the parking lot. "Just take it slow. There's no hurry."

At his vehicle, a white flyer was stuck under his wiper blade. As Abby retrieved it, William unlocked his vehicle to strap Carson into Ella's car seat.

Carson stiffened like he had on the ride over. "I don't like pink."

"I know. But it's a quick trip, Champ. Your mom's not feeling well, so we have to man up and do what it takes to help her get better. That means getting her home. And that means sitting in a pink seat."

Carson eyed him, his gaze full of doubt. Then his chest puffed out a bit, and he clambered into the seat and nattered to himself. "Haffa take care of Mommy. I be a man."

William glanced at Abby, hoping she'd seen her son's chivalrous sacrifice, but the color had drained from her face. She clenched the flyer in her fist.

"Abby?" He finished buckling Carson into his vehicle and took the paper from her. He smoothed it out and read the scrawled text. He wasn't an expert, but the penmanship looked similar to the note they'd found previously at the cottage. His stomach cemented.

Go home before someone else gets hurt.

A million emotions shot to the surface. The one that

surprised William the most was the protectiveness he felt for Abigail Sinclair.

Wordlessly, Abby climbed into the front seat of his car and clipped her seat belt together. Her shoulders rounded forward.

William battled conflicting feelings. He wanted to comfort her, assure her she'd be okay, pull her into a hug and let her know she wasn't alone. Any good human would do those things. But he was her employer, not a friend. He had no right to change the dynamics of their relationship. He held his tongue and followed her lead. He got into the car. They'd call the police from home.

Except it wasn't her home. It was his. William prayed that taking her there would be good enough for whoever left the threat. He backed out of the parking spot. His chest ached, and his eyes burned.

William stuck his phone in the built-in holder and drove on autopilot. His thoughts whipped through his mind as fast as the trees lining the ditch. Abby stared out the window.

It had been years since he'd ridden in a car like this. A woman beside him and a child in the back. It surprised him to discover it no longer stung. He was finally healing.

They continued in silence, each taken up with their thoughts until a notification popped on his phone screen.

Unknown tracking device located nearby.

Abby furrowed her brow. A vertical wrinkle appeared between her eyes. "What's that mean?"

William dismissed the notification. "It's a new thing on some phones. It runs through the lost phone feature and tracks belongings. I use it for my luggage when I travel."

"Why is it notifying you now?"

William turned into his driveway and followed the

winding path to the main house and parked. He cut the engine. "I'm not sure. Every compatible device gets a notification when an unknown electronically tagged item is out of the owner's range."

Abby made a funny noise in her throat. She fumbled with the car door, her panic contagious. A sense of urgency shot fire through his veins as she shrugged out of her cardigan and shook it. After patting herself down, she yanked open Carson's door and snatched his knapsack from the backseat. She hauled out item after item and dropped them on the ground.

"No, Mommy!"

She ignored Carson. "Did anyone approach you and Carson at the hospital?"

"No." He stood behind her now.

"No one bumped into you?"

"No—" Wait, that wasn't right. "Someone knocked Carson while we were walking back to the hospital room."

Her face tightened. "Carson, did anyone speak to you while you waited in the hall?"

William collected the discarded clothing, packaged snacks, and toys.

"A doctor said hi."

"How did you know he was a doctor?"

"He wore blue pajamas."

Scrubs. William scraped a hand down his face. Anyone could put on scrubs and pretend to be a doctor. He should never have left Carson in the hall.

Abby's frenzied movements stilled. Between her thumb and index finger, she held up a tiny device. "Someone tracked Carson."

FOUR

"Can you walk a bit longer?" Abby laced her fingers together behind her back in a casual posture, but she was ready to spring into action should Robert need her. The firm earth under their feet posed little threat to Robert's stability, but it only took one stray rock or knobby tree root to send a person tumbling. She'd mastered the art of being ready without looking ready a long time ago. A lifetime of running half marathons and road races kept her in top shape. It enabled her to make the physical aid she offered clients look effortless. Patients—men especially—didn't want to see a woman huffing and puffing trying to rescue them. Their limitations didn't matter as much if they continued to feel masculine.

"I think I can walk more." Robert shuffled at a pace Carson would have doubled. But it wasn't about speed. It was about progress. And considering that the man had fainted and fallen on the stairs only one week prior, she admired the old guy's determination.

Abby stopped and brushed her fingertips against the fuzzy skin of some low-hanging fruit. An unexpected shiver rippled down her spine. She couldn't explain it except to say it felt like someone was watching them. The hair on the back of her neck lifted. Peach trees stretched as far as she could see in organized rows. Nothing appeared out of order, but dread pooled in her belly.

She gave her head a shake. It was the tracking chip. She'd called Officer Reuben and he'd said there wasn't much they could do about the chip she'd found on Carson. But he advised her to stay alert. Something strange was going on, and somehow, she'd stepped into the middle of it the night she'd arrived.

Abby monitored Robert from the corner of her eye. When it looked like he'd caught his breath, she started to stroll again, pointing them toward Rose and the kids. Rose had spread a sizeable checkered blanket on the lawn, and the kids played with cardboard bricks, building walls and towers and knocking them down. Dreyfuss lay a few feet away. The mother in her wanted to snatch Carson up and disappear, leaving the danger behind. But she needed this job. She burned bridges leaving her last placement. There was little chance her former employer would give her a good reference when her decision to report the employee stealing meds had surrounded his facility in scandal.

Abby gave a wide berth to the beehives along the perimeter of the farm.

"They aid in pollination," Robert said, reading her mind.

"That's interesting." The more she learned about the farm and the more she learned about Robert, the better she'd understand his struggles.

Thick green leaves moved with the breeze, and the tree

limbs bent under growing fruit. None of the peaches dotted the ground yet, but by late August, the kids would be collecting the fallen "seconds" to sell at the roadside stand Rose had told her about. Carson couldn't wait.

Her belly flipped. Would they still be here then? After dealing with the police—for what felt like the millionth time in a matter of days—she was ready to pack it in. The officers had come up empty on the attack at the hospital. Whoever targeted them avoided the cameras in the hospital halls. Police leaned toward linking the events to the trouble from Abby's former workplace, but they didn't have enough evidence to be sure. Her former employer had been angry about all the bad press Abby had sent his way. It nearly destroyed his business. It didn't matter the owner was innocent. The social media courts had found him guilty of negligence.

It wasn't long after the details hit the press, the threats started to arrive. Abby had no problem believing her old boss was trying to intimidate her, but she didn't think he'd go so far as to actually hurt her. He just wanted her out of town so the whole mess could blow over.

But what if it wasn't connected? What if she'd just exchanged one nightmare for another—and dragged Carson straight into the middle of it? No job was worth risking his safety. But she'd signed a contract and already spent the signing bonus on the movers and their cut-short weekend visit to Austin and Sandy. If she broke the contract, she'd have to pay it back, and she didn't have the money. Besides, without this job, how would she keep a roof over Carson's head?

And it wasn't all about her. The more she listened to Robert, the more she believed he needed more than a PSW.

He needed a bodyguard. He and William just didn't know it yet. That was something her police background uniquely qualified her to provide, as long as protecting the elderly man didn't endanger her son.

"Tell me about the orchard. What was it like when you and your wife ran the place?" She tried to imagine it in its former days before all the heavy farm machinery came into use.

Long grass, wet with dew, swished against their pant legs as they strolled along the edge of the farm. She'd carefully tucked their pant hems into their boots to protect their skin from ticks. If only it were that easy to protect them from danger. To their right were rows of trees. To their left stood the main house with its expansive covered deck wrapped around all sides and a beckoning porch swing in need of fresh paint. The quaint cottage was almost ready for her and Carson's return, and a sprawling green lawn separated the two buildings. Several smaller cabins dotted the perimeter. Slowly, the creepy feeling that they had an audience lifted.

"It was a different time, a different world. But my Ruth managed it all. You would have loved her."

"Tell me about Ruth."

Robert's eyes grew dewy and soft. "She loved the smell of the orchard in the morning. The dirt and mulch, grass and fruit. Heaven's perfume, she called it. She was a firecracker, my Ruth. Like you."

Abby chuckled. She'd been called worse. By the time she'd pulled up the tent pegs and moved here, she'd been called every colorful name in the book by her former co-worker, who'd been arrested. Her boss had lost tens of thousands of dollars from the bad press, lawsuits, and family members removing their loved ones from care. Abby hadn't fully appreciated the linchpin she'd pulled until the dominoes fell. "Firecracker is far more complimentary than the recent expletives attached to my name."

"You chase justice, and when a person does that, they're bound to set off explosives and get called a few names." Robert missed little for a man everyone claimed to be regressing.

Name-calling, she could handle. As former police, she was used to it. But when the threats arrived, she pulled out. If anything happened to her, Carson would be all alone. She knew what that was like. She lost her parents, and she would not allow history to repeat itself in Carson's life. It was the reason she quit the police. It was the reason she moved here. And somehow, she landed in the middle of a mess anyway.

Robert lifted his chin toward her cottage. "I used to sit on that porch and chew my tobacco and smoke my cigars. Ruth wouldn't have it in the main house. You know, we lived there before we built the big house."

The idea of an old-school farm woman banishing her husband outdoors to smoke made her smile.

A squeal sounded from several yards away. Robert followed her gaze to the children. "They won't try again so soon."

"Who?"

"Whoever is trying to hurt me. They'll settle down now for a bit."

She furrowed her brow and stopped walking. But what about who was trying to hurt her? The canopy of trees filtered the sunlight, and a shiver zipped up her spine. Abby rubbed her upper arms. The fear was back, clinging to her like sweat after a run. "How do you know that?"

Robert's eyes flashed, clear and sharp. "It's the pattern."

This wasn't a muddled man. Not at this moment. He stood as tall as his fragile body would let him. He was every inch the leader and protector he used to be in his prime. She slipped her hands into the pockets of her long sweater. "Tell me about the pattern."

He hooked his thumbs through his front belt loops and started to walk again. "No one believes an old man, but I ain't crazy."

She matched his long legs, stride for stride. "I don't think you're crazy. I think you're in trouble."

"I thought once I got outta there, I'd be okay."

"Out of where?"

"Forget it." Robert's eyes shuttered. "You think I'm bonkers. I can see it on your face." The trees rustled and groaned.

"I don't, Robert, really. I'm just trying to understand. Help me understand."

"Them shakes Rose makes me started to taste funny. And right about then, my mind got fuzzy. I said something to Willy, and it went back to normal."

"Someone could have added something to your shakes and then pulled back when William looked into it," she mused. They'd have to be in the house or have a way to listen in on conversations to know when to pull back. But how much truth was woven through the conspiracy theories Robert spun? How much was imagination? How much were the effects of aging on a creative and paranoid mind?

"It happened at the nursing home, too."

"Chenaniah Manor? How long were you there?"

"Long enough," he huffed.

"Tell me about it."

"At first, it was good. But things got tough once they lost staff."

Abby got that. There was a health crisis in Ontario. Most government-run homes and hospitals were horribly under-staffed, and the employees that remained were overworked and underpaid.

"More people came to die, but they never increased the staff."

"What do you mean by *came to die*?"

"Kids talk about parents living in a nursing home. But the staff talk about patients dying in one."

Her gut twisted. Once that mindset grabbed hold, care went dramatically downhill. If death was inevitable, why bother? She clenched her jaw until her pulse throbbed in her temples. She knew the nursing home she outed wasn't the only place cutting corners. She might not be a cop anymore, but the mindset never turned off.

"I ain't crazy," Robert groused. "Some of the residents were in excruciating pain. And it only got worse."

"I believe you." It was a simple statement, but it changed everything.

Robert eyed her carefully and slowly nodded his head. "You really do. Thank you."

"Increased pain is expected in some health cases. Espe-cially if the home is the last stop before death. But it should be manageable."

Robert nodded along.

"Some coroners fail to look closely at the bodies from long-term homes if there are no red flags. There is an assumption that death is natural at that age."

"Ain't nothing natural about what I saw. For the longest

time, Willy never saw it. But one day he visited, and I was home before I could blink."

She smiled.

"Willy said he did it for me, but I think he did it for Ella." Robert's eyes found his great-granddaughter. "She's a beauty. Looks just like my Ruth."

"What do you mean he did it for Ella?"

"Ella needed a change. A place where everything and everyone didn't remind her of her mom. And Willy needed it too. He moved me home and moved his family here to take care of me."

They'd walked full circle and were back near the blanket where they had started with Rose and the kids.

"The children want their stuffed toys. Do you mind if I go inside and get them?" Rose asked.

Nothing moved in the treeline. There was no reason for the trepidation rolling in the pit of her stomach. Abby forced a smile. "If Robert is okay with staying out longer, it's fine with me. We can watch the kids."

Robert smiled indulgently at the children. "They can tell me about this structure they're building."

Rose hurried off, and Abby watched her go as she set up a folding chair for Robert. Rose was very agile for her age. Abby hoped she aged as well as the seasoned woman.

Gramps sat down, and she squatted before him to massage his calf muscles. They got pretty tight after a walk.

Robert snapped his fingers at his side, and Dreyfuss moved in. He sat beside Robert like a dog at attention. The local guy who trained Dreyfuss did a fabulous job.

Abby's phone vibrated, alerting her to an incoming text message. She slipped her hand into her pocket and tipped the phone just enough for her to see the screen. An image appeared. Gramps on the chair. The kids on the blanket. Abby at Robert's feet. Along with the caption: *I could kill him right now.*

WILLIAM TRAILED a few yards behind Rose, who clutched Ella's stuffed dog and Carson's teddy in her arms as she hurried back to the kids. She'd come to the house, humming a hymn of God's faithfulness. She told him about their impromptu picnic on the lawn as she passed his open office door, and William impulsively decided he needed some sunshine and laughter. A break would do his mind and heart good. He hadn't been able to figure out the books anyway.

Peach trees dotted with green fruit grew in rows as long as the eye could see. He'd never tire of the view. Abby's cottage was tucked into the property like a baby bird under its mother's wing. There was something very quaint and perfect about the orchard, paint-it-on-a-canvas kind of perfect. Overwhelming thankfulness that made his chest swell was followed quickly by fear. What if he couldn't save it? What if his efforts came too late to turn the ship sailing toward bankruptcy?

Ella laughed, and his gaze zipped to his daughter. She giggled at something Carson had said, her face bright and animated. The May breeze carried her bubbly voice but muffled her words. But he didn't need words to understand. She clasped her hands to her chest, her tone communicating a settledness that she'd previously lacked. Lightness filled his limbs. He had to save the orchard. If not for Gramps, then for Ella.

After Claire died, Ella became so lethargic that William had actually feared she'd die from a broken heart. That downward spiral nudged William into pulling Ella from everything familiar to move them to the orchard. He'd acted with false confidence. He'd begged God for wisdom and agonized in prayer. But God didn't reveal the next twelve months or even the next season. God had only clarified that moving home was the next step. The joy bubbling from his daughter now confirmed his decision. He had to trust the Lord had a plan for their financial issues as well.

Taking that leap of obedience had been one of the hardest things he'd ever done. The obstacles didn't part for him as they did for Moses when he stepped into the water. The orchard was still in financial trouble. Ella still had nightmares. He still ached with loneliness. But he got up each day and found God's new mercies strong enough for him. He had one plan. Follow God.

Who led him right to Abby.

Abby had proved to be more than her resume had promised. Not only was she the health care professional Gramps needed, but her female presence lifted Ella's spirits. Last night, Ella had even restarted an old tradition. At bedtime, she'd recapped her day to William. They chose three great things and one not-so-great thing about the day so they could pray and give thanks to the Lord. William had let the habit fall away when Ella had fixated on the negative and refused to see any good. But last night, she started again, all on her own. It lifted a weight that he hadn't even realized was crushing him. Ella was finding the good again, and she found it in Abby.

The way Abby fit into their family so seamlessly startled him. Every time Abby's hand rested on Ella's shoulder or she pressed it against the girl's back in the ordinary way adults interacting with children often did, Ella's face glowed with such longing that his chest ached. It differed from how his daughter looked at Rose. Ella loved Rose, but it was the sort of love that developed between a grandmother and a grand-daughter. It was different with Abby. More motherly. It happened naturally because of Carson. Contradiction chopped at his insides. Part of him welcomed the change in Ella, but another part braced against it. She'd been hurt too many times already. The police had finally released the cottage, so he should feel relieved. Rose could start putting it back together for Abby, and he and Ella could regain their personal space. But that meant Abby and Carson would move from the main house, and Ella would feel that absence sharply. William prayed for wisdom and for Ella's protection. She wouldn't survive another loss.

A primal scream ripped through his mulling, chilling his blood.

Abby shot to her feet. She yanked the kids up by their arms. "Get inside!"

William started to run.

Gramps pushed to his feet, unsteady, eyes bulging. Drey-fuss stiffened, eyes on his master.

"But I don't wanna—" Carson didn't have time to finish the sentence. Abby shoved her son toward the house, and he stumbled and cried.

Dreyfuss barked and circled Gramps.

"Run!"

Ella latched onto Abby's leg and refused to let go.

Rose reached them first. Abby peeled off Ella, thrust her toward Rose, and said something William couldn't hear. Rose clutched Ella, who'd buried her face in Rose's shoulder. Her little body heaved with cries.

Rose spun and hurried toward the main house as fast as

she could. She scooped up Carson's hand on the way. The earlier confusion on her face transformed into terror. "Go back to the house, Mr. William!"

"Daddy!" Ella reached for him as he neared.

Not stopping for Ella was the hardest thing he'd ever done. "Get the kids inside. I'm getting Gramps."

Abby struggled to support Gramps. Dreyfuss whimpered and paced. William couldn't hear Abby's words, but the hard lines on her face and Gramps's determination said enough. Each step closer increased his clarity.

Threat.

Shooter.

Hurry!

His heartbeat thrashed in his ears.

Gramps shoved Abby's hands away. "Kids—"

"I'm not leaving you."

Abby looped one arm around Gramps's waist. She craned her neck and stared into the trees. Her wild eyes finally found William's. Her nostrils flared.

There wasn't time for details. He slipped his arm around Gramps and shifted the man's weight to him. "I've got him. You help Rose with the kids."

The flat-out terror on her face petrified him.

Abby bolted toward the children.

"Protect," William commanded Dreyfuss.

Dreyfuss sprinted after the children and Rose. He ran a circle around them, herding them toward safety.

Abby took Carson. Rose still clutched Ella. If Gramps's bones weren't so fragile, William would have tossed the man over his shoulder in a similar fashion. But as it was, he could only pray that they weren't in a gun's scope.

The tendons in Gramps's neck popped out. His elbows

pressed into his sides, making it harder to support him. He stared ahead blankly. His breath burst in and out. Gramps was going into shock.

"Just a little further." William coaxed him and prayed for protection, one step at a time.

Carson pounded on his mother, but she didn't break stride.

It was all over in about sixty seconds.

William and Gramps were the last to reach the house. He slammed the front door behind them and twisted the lock. He helped Gramps to the nearest seat. Abby handed a resistant Carson to Rose, who had backed into a corner.

Abby pulled the curtains closed. Gramps wheezed and coughed but didn't complain. The children whimpered. They'd all collapsed in various places. Ella crawled to William, and he scooped her up. She clung to him like she did the day of her mother's funeral. Like she'd never let go. Her tears dampened his shoulder.

William threw a blanket over Gramps's legs with his free hand. Some of the color was returning to his cheeks. Abby had filled a glass with water and handed it to him, her hand trembling, dribbling the water over the cup's rim.

"What happened?"

Abby's chest heaved.

Ella shifted and nuzzled into his neck. He pressed his lips to the top of her head. The faint aroma of sweat drifted upward.

Abby held out her phone for him to see the screen.

The image blurred.

He sank onto the nearest chair before lightheadedness could weaken his knees. Ella refused to let go, so he adjusted her on his lap. Him. The writer had written shoot *him*. The only males in the image were Carson and Gramps. "I'm calling the police." William was already dialing.

"Bear-be," Carson wept. "I want Bear-be."

Rose handed him to Carson, but his wails only increased. "He's broken!"

Abby took the toy and turned it over, and a rip in the back seam opened. "We'll sew him up," she promised.

A torn bear was the least of their troubles.

Abby stiffened. She lifted the toy closer, her features pinching together. "There's something inside."

She shoved her hand through the opening. With widening eyes, she withdrew a small package of capsules and lifted a pale face to his. "It's drugs."

CHAPTER

FIVE

rugs? This was about drugs? Abby rubbed her eyelids. Her mind flashed back to the highway rest stop. Carson had dropped the bear, or so she'd thought. Could their Good Samaritan have planted the drugs before returning the toy? But why?

She scrunched her face, digging for the memory. The man had made her uncomfortable. He'd seemed overly familiar. Unkempt. Early thirties. Jeans at least a full size too large that he constantly hiked up. Dark eyes. No, she pressed her lips together. Dark circles under his eyes. Like he was tired. He looked like he'd had a rough time. Was maybe even homeless. But she'd assumed the red tint in the whites of his eyes indicated a long-haul trucker.

But the police officer had searched him. The image of the man up against the cruiser and submitting to a pat-down filled her mind.

If the search turned up empty, the officer would have been forced to release him. Did he follow her to the cottage?

She tried to remember the feel of the person she'd fought off. Had he been lanky or thick? She spread her thumb and forefinger across her forehead and stretched the skin. *Think!* Someone had planted drugs on her baby. Was she just in the wrong place at the wrong time, targeted out of convenience?

A stream of questions from William interrupted her thoughts. "Where did the drugs come from? How did they get into the bear? Where did you buy the bear?"

She fingered the baggie in her hands. The pills rolled between her fingertips and thumb. Wait. She manipulated a single tablet to see the logo stamped on it. She'd seen this before.

"Abby?" William practically shouted now. He was still on the phone with the police, relaying information.

Her eyes popped open. "It's a chemist Austin and I put away years ago." Either the chemist was pressing pills again or someone new took over the operation. "I need to call Austin."

"You need to explain."

Abby registered her surroundings. Ella whimpered. Carson cried for her, reaching out his arms. Rose clenched him, her own tears spilling down her cheeks.

Abby would give almost anything to have the luxury of holding Carson close and promising him everything would be okay. But she couldn't. She couldn't afford the distraction of his fear. Their lives depended on her clear head.

"The drugs explain the attacks and the tracking chip," she said. "But not the attack on Robert. Robert's the outlier." She stuck a pin in the detail that didn't fit and pulled back the edge of the curtain to peek outside. She didn't see anybody. She let the drapes fall back into place. "An officer looking for drugs wouldn't look twice at a mother traveling with a small child.

Especially a former cop." Her rage intensified as she connected the dots, and blood pulsed in her ears. Anger wouldn't help. She needed to think. She checked the back door. Locked. Felt all the tabs on the windows as she passed them.

William trailed behind her. Poking. Prodding. Demanding answers she couldn't provide. She clenched the package and held in the guttural roar building internally. "Whoever hid this on Carson wants it back." And he had them cornered. "How long until the police arrive?"

"They're on the way." William listened to something the dispatcher was saying before speaking again. "She wants to know if there is anywhere safe we can wait?"

"We can go to the cellar," Rose suggested.

"Get moving," Abby commanded.

William put Ella down in front of Rose. "Don't let anyone in unless you're certain they are the police."

With a hand from each child in hers, Rose hurried to the basement.

Dreyfuss moved closer to Gramps, who pulled himself shakily to his feet. Abby looped an arm around his waist. When William didn't follow, she turned back. "You coming?"

William didn't answer. His expression contorted.

She sent Robert ahead. "William?"

He extended the phone to Abby, and as she reached for it with her free hand, he snatched the pills from her.

"What are you doing?"

William was already out the front door with the baggie held high. He might as well paint a target on his head. The porch boards rattled under William's feet. Spittle flew from the corners of his mouth. "You threaten a kid? Is this what you want? Come and get it, you coward."

Abby grabbed his upper arm. "Get back inside," she hissed. "Wait for the police."

A tiny voice from the phone in her hand instructed them not to engage with the suspect.

William shrugged off her clammy grip and ran toward his vehicle. He yanked open the driver's door and tossed the package onto the backseat. He glared at Abby. "This ends today. Tell the police I'm bringing the pills to them. Whoever wants them will follow me."

This was crazy. Reckless and foolish. "No, William, don't."

The voice coming through the phone speakers got louder. "Do not engage."

"Keep the kids safe," William said.

She felt for her weapon, momentarily forgetting she had given it up when she changed careers. *Lord, help me.*

Every fiber of her being wanted to stand guard over Carson, but William revved the engine. She dove into the passenger side. William had one thing right. The trouble would follow the pills.

His pulse throbbed in his neck; the tendons engorged. Sweat beaded on his upper lip. "We have to get it away from the kids."

"This is former Officer Abigail Sinclair," Abby spoke with authority. "Someone planted street drugs on my son. They've threatened us. The housekeeper took the kids and Robert Roth into the basement. They locked themselves in the cellar. I'm with William Roth in his car. We're coming to the station."

William ripped out of the driveway. Abby braced her hands on the dashboard as they careened around a corner.

"Shelter in place," the operator said. "Officers are on their way."

"Too late," Abby said. "We're on our way."

The operator's tone changed. "Are you being followed?"

An engine roared from somewhere behind them. William's eyes bulged.

"Yes." Her gut bottomed out. *Lord, I don't want to leave Carson an orphan.*

She knew all too well what that kind of life meant for him.

"Describe the vehicle."

"It's a black SUV. Tinted windows. Newer model. The driver is young." Abby squinted. Baby faced. Determined. Abby couldn't see his eyes. Despite all her training, fear for Carson had stripped her of detail. All she saw was his sneer. He wasn't backing off.

"I've dispatched a unit to meet you on the road. Can you stay on the line?"

"For as long as we can." She clenched her jaw. Ditches dropped on either side of them. The vehicle behind them crept closer, and expecting a bump from it, William twisted the steering wheel and merged onto a dirt side road. An arc of dirt sprayed.

The car followed, but they'd gained some space.

"What's your route?"

Abby glanced at William.

"We're on Gardner's Lane to Rest Acres," he mumbled, finally finding his voice. He slowed a touch and cranked the wheel. The little sedan lifted as it cornered and settled back down with a thud. The package shot across the backseat.

"Where did you learn to drive like this?"

William's knuckles whitened. "He's still following us."

"I know," Abby forced the words through clenched teeth. She pressed her lips together. William just needed to hold on a little longer. If the police were coming toward them as fast as they were heading their way, they'd intersect any second, and it would all be over. The guy would back off to avoid capture when the sirens and police lights hit. While he changed direction, the police would overtake him.

"ETA two minutes," the operator said.

Two minutes. William only needed to hold on for two minutes. Then, whoever was after them would know they no longer had the drugs. Carson would be safe. They'd all go back to normal life. That's all that mattered.

"Where are you now?" the dispatcher asked.

"Rest Acres to Main and Main to Pleasant Valley." William's voice raised in pitch.

William shouldn't have done this. It was stupid. Abby clutched the seat belt that cut across her chest and braced herself against the door frame as he cornered again, getting back on a main road. Her lip twitched. Her hands cramped from gripping the seat belt, but she didn't let up. William passed a slow-moving car, laying on the horn as he crossed the yellow line. He crested the hill and swerved back to his side of the road, handling the vehicle perfectly.

"The officers should be on the scene any second," the dispatcher said.

The SUV passed the car behind them, rushed forward, and tapped their back end. They fishtailed. William cranked the wheel right, then left, steering out of the near spin.

"We might not have that long." William floored it up another incline.

As they crested the top, red lights flashed. The tension in her shoulders released a smidge. William's grip on the steering wheel relaxed for a millisecond. It was almost over. Everybody was going to be okay.

She looked at William, expecting to see relief. His bulging eyes didn't blink. His breath rasped in, and he recoiled and slammed the brakes.

She jerked her gaze back. "No, no, no, no, no!"

The squeal of brakes assaulted their ears. Dirt billowed around them. The scene unfolded in painful slow motion.

A yellow school bus. Stopped traffic. Flashing lights. Extended rail. Bobbing heads of children. Kids spilling from the open door.

Car horns wailing.

People screaming.

The brakes couldn't compete with the vehicle's momentum.

Everything narrowed to one lifted face barely visible over the car's hood.

Her little eyes wide and terrified.

William cranked the wheel.

A primitive screech peeled from Abby's lungs. *"Noooooo!"*

THE HORIZON TIPPED. A blow slammed into William's chest. A hard stop. The thrust forced the air from his lungs. His breath rocketed out.

Please, Lord.

Everything screamed with grinding, shattering glass, and rubber on dirt. Then quiet.

No, that wasn't right.

Faint screams grew in intensity and volume. William's fuzzy head cleared. The car had rolled but eventually landed right side up. It rocked. Was he hurt? The deflating airbag released a steady hiss.

"Are you okay?" A faint voice sounded from somewhere near his feet. "Is anyone hurt?"

His phone. Abby dropped it.

Abby.

His neck twinged as he turned his head. Abby slapped at the airbag in front of her, looking as stunned and confused as he felt. They were okay. Alive.

Relief collided with fear.

The bus? The kids? Oh, God, please, no.

Who was screaming?

He fought against whatever held him back. His clumsy hands fumbled with the door handle. Why was everything hazy? He couldn't get out. He shoved his shoulder against the door. They couldn't get out! Why couldn't he get out?

Abby's lips moved, but he couldn't hear her. His mouth dried, and his windpipe narrowed. His vision disfigured. He pressed the heel of his palm to his chest. Was he having a heart attack?

Abby reached across the car and cut the engine, but it still hissed and popped.

Pressure across his core registered. His seat belt! He fumbled for the latch, his fingers fat and clumsy. Finally, his thumb slid over the button, and he pushed down, freeing himself. The roar in his ears lessened.

"Are you okay?" Abby's eyes clouded. With pain or confusion?

"I think so."

He unlocked her seat belt.

Several people spilled into the ditch. "Are you all right in there?" Palms pounded on his window.

On Abby's side, a hand reached in and touched her shoulder. She jerked.

What happened to her window? What if it was the guy following them? How would they know? Would he be so brazen?

"We're okay." William focused on the face of Abby's rescuer. He couldn't tell if he'd been driving the SUV.

William's muscles seized and pressure caved in from all sides. The air felt too thin to sustain him. His panicky breath grew shallow and sped up. Darkness crept in at the corners of his vision.

Abby slapped the stranger's hand away. "The bus! The kids—"

The man working on her jammed door paused. He stooped. The kindness in his eyes nearly undid William. This was not their pursuer.

Please, Lord. Let everyone be okay.

"Everybody's safe out here. You didn't hit anyone."

Abby sagged.

Pressure shot up his throat. William wanted to sob. Not just tears, but wails. He fought for control, still his entire body pitched and his extremities tingled. His beating heart lodged in his throat, and he couldn't swallow it.

Someone nearby was moaning and crying, too.

It wasn't Abby.

Abby's head had tipped back, and her eyes closed. Her tense facial muscles relaxed as if someone had thrown a blanket of calm over her. It was like she was sleeping.

"Keep those eyes open, lady," the kind man's tone sharpened. "We gotta get you outta here, and I need your help." He gently shook Abby.

She jerked. Rousing and slapping his hands simultaneously. Then she blinked several times and nodded. She puckered. Swallowed. And forced herself up.

And he struggled to breathe. It was hard. Really hard. He squeezed his eyes closed and focused. The heaving slowed. He pulled his sleeve across his face, wiping his nose.

The engine smoked. A weird pinging, like water hitting hot metal, repeated. Out. They had to get out. Would they be safe out there?

He sucked in a shuddering breath. More bodies gathered on his side of the vehicle. Hands wrenched the bent door and forced it open. Slow motion morphed into time jumps.

They were out of the car and had climbed up the ditch. Kids clung to their caregivers. Tears. Cries. White faces and horror.

But no blood. Thank you, Jesus. There was no blood.

William's knees gave way. He collapsed, and Abby sank beside him. They hadn't spoken to each other beyond their initial assurances that they were alive.

Police cars arrived, screaming and flashing. The vehicle chasing them, the one idling a distance away surveilling the scene, turned and left.

Nobody noticed but him.

An ambulance announced its impending arrival. Firetruck tires crunched on the dirt road. Officers headed their way.

Abby dragged herself to her feet, arms folded over her midsection.

He remained on the ground. His legs turned to jelly.

Abby motioned to their vehicle in the ditch. He only caught a few disjointed words to the officers. His ears still hummed. *Drugs. Planted. Coming to the station.*

His adrenaline dropped. A chill swept up his spine. He'd

left his phone in the car. Was the operator still calling his name? He should get the phone. Tell her they were okay.

The tremors started small. He needed to get away. He needed Ella. He needed—*O God, I need You. Thank you. Thank you. Thank you.*

Another uncontrollable cry welled up. He turned his back to the chaos, trying to hold back the waves rolling in. How was Abby upright and talking? How was she functioning? His body shook. *Thank you, Lord, for protecting the kids. That no one is hurt. That we are alive.*

Ten seconds ago, he'd been ready to stand by Abby's side and face their pursuers with the strength of a superhero. Now, he tried to hide his weakness from the onlookers. From Abby.

"Are you ready, sir?" A young officer William didn't recognize tapped him gently. Wisdom far beyond the young man's years emanated. He seemed to understand the aftermath of a tragedy. He waited patiently for William to pull it together.

"Yeah," William finally croaked.

The officer squatted beside William, getting that he wasn't ready to stand upright. "Can you tell me what happened?"

The officer's radio constantly interrupted William's recap of the events leading up to the crash, but he remained sensitive and kind and attentive. He also emitted a strange seriousness that multiplied an overwhelming giddiness in William.

"Can you repeat your question?" William massaged his forehead. His hand shook with tiny tremors that he seemed unable to control. He flexed his fingers. Nope. Still shaking.

Shock must be setting in. He fisted them in his lap, his trimmed nails cutting into his flesh.

Patience oozed out of the officer. He repeated himself.

Before William could answer, everything began to ache. First, his neck. It spread to his back and out from his center until every nerve ending in his body throbbed. He sucked in a breath. Something wasn't right.

"Are you okay?" The officer furrowed his brow.

"Everything hurts."

He lifted his arm and flagged a medic. "Can you do this now?"

William pinched his eyes closed. He nodded. "We were being chased. Abby was on the line with 911." Didn't the operator update the police? Didn't they know what was happening? Anger surged through him, momentarily dulling the pain. "Did you get him?"

The officer looked up from his notepad. "Who?"

"The guy following us. He broke into my cottage. He threatened my family." His voice cracked. His muscles quivered.

The medic dropped to his side. "You need to stay calm, sir."

Anger surged. "You have to make sure the kids are safe!" Spittle flew from his lip. Abby's eyes found his from where she stood speaking with the first responders. She started his way. Slowly. With a hitch in her gait. His pulse hiked. She could have been killed. Heat rushed through him.

"Officers are looking for him right now," the officer said. "Others went to your house. My job is to hear from you. Learn what happened."

The medic opened his bag.

William stopped. He drew a slow, controlled breath. Losing his temper would help no one. It took all his focus to maintain control. Doubts filled him. Had he done something wrong? Should he have stayed at the house? Was this his fault?

"Your wife is fine, sir." The medic misunderstood William's angst. But he also seemed to understand that anger was the next step in William's grief.

William never corrected his assumption.

Then, Abby was there. It was all he needed to find the strength to get to his feet.

"I'm okay, William." Abby blinked fast, but not fast enough to hide her pain. Her gaze was a mirror of all that reeled inside of him.

His inhalation shuddered. "For real?"

"Yes."

He reached out. Slowly at first. Gently. Unsure of the appropriateness of his actions but desperately needing the contact for his mental health. He blew out his cheeks and swallowed air. He needed something only she could give him.

When she didn't pull back, he folded her into his arms.

She threaded her arms around his middle and pressed her cheek against his chest. He released a slow breath, finally able to breathe.

He tipped his chin down. The scent of her shampoo drifted up. Dampness covered his cheeks. Her entire frame trembled.

"I'll come back later." The officer stepped away.

The medic simply waited.

William hadn't held a woman in his arms since Claire died. Until now, the idea of it felt wrong. Unfaithful even. But as he steadied Abby, something in the weight of her grief pulled at his own. The familiar heaviness in his chest shifted —not gone, but shared. Claire no longer needed him; she had the wholeness of eternity in the Lord's presence. But Abby stood here, flesh and blood, carrying burdens she could not carry alone. And for the first time in a long while, he felt useful again.

Tomorrow, he might call this moment a mistake. Tomorrow, he might wish he'd kept a careful distance. But today, none of that mattered. Today, someone needed him and he refused to step back.

CHAPTER
SIX

Abby wrapped both hands around a steaming mug and lifted it to her face. A caramelized, nutty aroma swaddled her in a hug. It had been one week since the accident, and her body still hurt. She was pretty sure that her bruises had bruises. Pain fogged her brain, but coffee would help.

She hadn't slept well, partly because Carson kept kicking her in his sleep and partly because she jumped at every sound. But she'd insisted Carson sleep with her. Not because Carson needed it, but because she did. And now she needed an IV drip of caffeine just to function.

Abby claimed the wingback chair by the front window. William sat in the adjacent chair.

"Where's Gramps?" William asked.

"Your Uncle Joe stopped in. They were visiting on the back porch when I left them." From this vantage point, Abby had a clear line of sight to the kids playing in the yard. Tension knotted her shoulders. Detective Reuben's search of the property provided little comfort. They'd come up with nothing that would help them get to the bottom of things. Andy had taken photographs and collected evidence and said figuring it out was going to take time.

Time they might not have.

All the police could say with certainty was that someone had been in the woods and none of the migrant workers had seen anything. Whether that someone had a gun was up for debate.

A hoot from outside pulled her attention. Rose had set up a cornhole game for the children, and they shrieked with delight. They remained totally oblivious of how close they'd come to losing their parents. For whatever reason, their tormentor had pulled back.

For now.

"No one is there." William answered her unasked question. "I had Dreyfuss run the perimeter."

Abby rubbed the middle of her forehead. William's reckless actions ensured that whoever was after them knew the police had the drugs. She didn't know whether to love him or hate him for running off the way he did. She lifted the mug to her lips instead of replying.

Her irrational core refused to release its coiled tension. Abby should quit. She should take Carson and run. Except the medic that treated her after the accident had cautioned her against making rash decisions over the next few days. He'd said that after trauma, the body sometimes responds as if the threat is still present. It tries to get you to flee.

But they were safe.

She repeated it like a chant, trying not to read into the tic twitching in William's jaw. *They were safe.* Besides, if she left, she had no place to go. No family to help. This job was literally all she and Carson had.

The dependency made her insides squirm.

William nursed his own mug of coffee. He'd made their drinks in the fancy stainless steel machine she'd noticed on the kitchen counter and didn't know how to use. His fingers cradled the ceramic, and he watched the children with intensity. Was he thinking along the same lines as her? That she brought a truckload of trouble to his family and she should go?

Her breath hiccuped. That wasn't the message she'd received at the accident scene. Heat prickled her cheeks as his steady grip replayed in her mind like muscle memory she couldn't shake. When he'd held her, she'd felt safe. Which made no sense. They'd only just met, and after everything that had happened, she should feel anything but secure. Yet William's presence pressed back against the chaos, if only for a moment. Her aches shifted deeper, into her soul. No one had steadied her like that since her parents. Maybe Austin and Sandy, at times. But never like this.

Right. She still had to call Austin and tell him about the drugs.

She cleared her throat, and William startled, as if the sound jolted him from deep thought. Her question scraped against her raw throat. "Do you think it's over?"

She had no idea what was happening in this household and why Gramps was sick all the time or whether the danger had truly passed or was just ramping up.

"Partly." The single word was loaded. "The break-in, clamp on the gas line, and the device on Carson were probably about the drugs." He pinched the bridge of his nose as his words trailed off. "But the hospital? Gramps? The notes and threatening messages? It doesn't make sense. Not yet."

She moistened her lips. Maybe the question swirling between them wasn't whether she should leave. Maybe the real question was whether he'd fire her if he thought she'd brought this trouble to his household. A lump choked off her air supply and painfully moved down her throat.

"I don't think it's done," he said. "I feel it in my gut."

His vulnerability surprised her. To date, he'd seemed nothing but capable. Completely certain. Determined even. But right now, he looked like Carson when he was scared.

"I found this shoved under the door." He held a paper between his index and middle fingers.

Trepidation crawled like bugs underneath her skin. Scrawled across the page was her name. She hated how her hand trembled as she reached for the note.

Go home.

Her lips went numb. She clenched her teeth against a roiling stomach.

William's gaze never left her face, invading her space despite sitting an entire end table away. He watched, giving her time. He didn't speak until she released her clenched jaw. "What do you want to do? Do you feel comfortable staying on here? I'd completely understand if you wanted to leave."

What did she want? She wanted a million things. She wanted her parents to come back. She wanted a multigenerational family to mentor her through adulthood. She wanted cousins for Carson and aunts and uncles. She wanted permanence and stability, but everyone she had ever loved had been taken from her. She was all Carson had, and whoever sent her this letter wanted to take her from him. But of course, she wasn't about to tell him any of that.

"I want to be safe."

He nodded, his features tight. He was too hard to read for her to know if he felt relief that she didn't give her notice. Hard enough that when he asked if he could pray for them, she snorted, and then tried to cover it with a cough.

She snorted. She didn't mean to. It just slipped out. She might walk out her faith in constant tension with the Lord, but evidence lay all over the house indicating William maintained a deeply meaningful relationship with God. Completed Bible studies, commentaries, and seminary-level textbooks filled the bookcases in the library. But none of that prepared her for an offer to pray together. Lots of academics studied the Bible as an ancient piece of literature and not as the living Word of God.

And praying together was *intimate.*

William extended his hand.

She slipped her smaller one into his. Her heart throbbed in her ears. It was just a prayer. It meant nothing. William's worn Bible on the table beside his chair revealed the depth of his faith. He sat in this chair every morning with a coffee, notebook, and pen, reading and reflecting on the Word before starting his day. God meant something to him, and *she snorted*, effectively dumping her spiritual baggage at his feet. She bowed her head.

"God, you are our protector, defender, and rescuer."

She desperately wanted to believe God was her protector. She didn't deny His existence. Nor did she challenge His right to rule His creation. Her upbringing had shaped a robust theology. But experience had taught her that God was distant. And police work had taught her a person needed to be near to protect you. It wasn't something you did from afar.

William asked God for wisdom and safety and ended with a simple request. "Father, please help us. Amen."

Help us. She liked the sound of *us*. Being a team. Working together. Not being the sole person responsible for everything, because despite how she pretended to handle whatever life threw her way, she didn't really believe she held control. But her pretense made her feel better. It made her feel like she had a say in what happened to her and that if something truly awful were to occur, she'd find a way to stop it.

She lifted her head at William's amen. His prayer was shorter than she expected and more direct. Their eyes connected, and his gaze emitted such tenderness that her chest pinched. "Do you really think God will give you a supernatural understanding of what's going on?"

"I think He will give me whatever I need, but I'm not wise enough to know what that is, so I'll wait and see what He does."

She pulled her hand from his, not understanding that kind of trust and patience because it felt like God had walked away from her. "Don't you worry?"

"Yes, but I trust the Lord."

"Why? You can sacrifice everything, do everything right, put others first, and there's still no guarantee that life will be safe." She thought of her parents.

"I think God's concern for me is larger than what keeps me physically safe."

"What's more important than safety?" Her gaze found the children again.

"Eternity."

It was simple. One word. Spoken with confidence. Yet it

slammed into her with the force of a gale wind. He sounded just like her dad.

"I lost my parents in a fire." She hadn't planned to tell him. It just came out.

He didn't respond. He sat quietly, letting her feel whatever she felt.

"I was out with a friend. It was my last year of high school. I was late getting home." She fiddled with the cuff of her sleeve, wishing with everything in her that she could go back in time and make different decisions. "When I arrived, the house was fully engulfed, and firefighters were battling it."

Still silent. She didn't dare meet his eyes. She didn't want to see the same expression she'd seen a million times, so she looked past him. First at the wall, then at the bookcase. Anywhere except his eyes. Because worse than seeing pity would be kindness and a willingness to enter her pain.

"People said all the churchy things. God is in control. He won't let you down. But if He was in control, why didn't He stop it? And if He's lost control, then I can't trust Him. Not with my life. Not with Carson." She finally let her gaze settle on his.

"What do you think God should have done?"

"Anything would have been better than nothing."

"I've wrestled with similar questions."

Yet his faith remained intact. William's eyes glazed as if he were rewatching history.

"Did you get an answer?" She was almost afraid to ask. She wasn't sure if she could handle another disappointment. Another Christian cliché that failed to reach her where she hurt.

"God's more interested in saving souls than removing suffering."

"I'm not sure that's a God I can trust."

"I'm sad to hear that."

And that was it. No lecture. No sermon about why she was wrong. He didn't even look uncomfortable. He let it sit between them with no need to challenge or correct it.

When she couldn't stand it any longer, she broke the silence. "How can you have such confidence in God?"

A thread of pain snaked across his face, but it didn't diminish the joy radiating from his eyes. "God loves me. I measure everything against that truth. If I don't, I'll misread my circumstances, and they will destroy me."

Did God love her? The question sat uncomfortably in her middle, where her doubts swirled.

SILENCE STRETCHED BETWEEN THEM. The kind William knew with Claire when she was alive. Each satisfied with the other's company and neither needing to fill the quiet. William's mind drifted back to his bookkeeping problem. For some reason, he couldn't make the numbers reconcile. He was transferring Gramps's on-paper ledger to a computer software program that was supposed to make things easier with its automated columns and figuring, but the numbers didn't add up. The discrepancy made him feel too hot and too cold all at once. And with all the extra *drama*, he hadn't had time to uncover the root issue.

He tapped his fingers on his thigh. His gaze zipped to the note Abby still held in her hand. Whoever sent it, whoever had targeted Abby, had been outside his home. Close to his daughter. Gramps. Near Carson and Rose. Again.

He scraped a hand over his face. Had the intruder not left a calling card, William would have never known of the danger. William would have carried on in full faith that his home was secure, and he'd have been wrong. Dangerously wrong.

What kind of caregiver missed people skulking about right under his nose?

His attention fell on the closed ledger resting on the table between them. The kind of person who let fruit farms go into foreclosure.

Okay. Not exactly foreclosure. But the place wasn't thriving.

"I have some concerns about Robert." Abby interrupted his internal dialogue and dragged him back into the present. She crossed one leg over the other.

William set his coffee down and rested his elbows on his knees.

"I'm concerned about Robert's overall weakness. The doctor shared Robert's medical file,"—she flicked her gaze to his—"with Robert's approval, of course." She folded her hands in her lap to stop her fidgeting. "There isn't any medical reason for the level of exhaustion he feels."

William frowned. "Isn't that part of the natural aging process? Wasn't that why you started the walks and the protein shakes? To rebuild his strength?"

"Yes, but those are treating the symptoms, not the cause. I'd like to figure out why he feels so weak. His nausea and confusion bother me. I've worked with a lot of elderly people. This doesn't feel like the usual slower pace. It feels different."

William ground his teeth together, letting up only when a shot of pain moved along his jaw. The list of things needing his attention kept growing, and Gramps's care came with a hefty price tag. Yet, no matter what William did, the accounts came up short every month. He didn't know how Uncle Joe had kept the place going. They'd already chewed through any financial cushion Gramps had squirreled away a long time ago.

It didn't help that the entire community assumed the orchard still rolled in cash. Various organizations asked for annual donations. What would people think if the place went belly up months after he stepped in? It wouldn't matter that he'd inherited a financial mess. The assumption would be that he ran the business into the ground.

Pain scorched the back of his throat. And there was Abby to consider. She depended on him. He was her livelihood. She moved here for this job. The job he wasn't sure he could continue to pay her for doing unless something changed. But that wasn't the reason for his discomfort. "You're not buying into his theories that the government is trying to kill him, are you?"

Laughter popped out.

William chuckled. "Asked and answered."

"I don't buy into his theories, but something is off. I can't put my finger on it. I just wanted you to know so that you could watch for anything out of the ordinary. I don't like how his symptoms seem to be gradually worsening despite the changes I've implemented to his routine."

"So I should be on the lookout for unusual things, like threatening notes and drugs?" He lifted an eyebrow and glanced pointedly at the note in her hand.

Red blushed her cheeks. "I'm thinking about things related specifically to him. Like his balance issues. That's new. And have you noticed the way his face flushes?"

Heat spread from the back of William's neck and crept up to his ears until the tips of them burned.

"It's okay if you haven't noticed," Abby said. "Most people would write those things off as age-related. But I don't think these are normal issues."

The warmth in Abby's voice ignited something in him he hadn't felt in years. A protective urge to steady her world and keep danger at bay. The feeling startled him. He fidgeted with his wedding band, rubbing the pad of his thumb over its rim. Had it been wise to invite her and Carson into the main house? But then he looked at the facts. Someone had ransacked the cottage. With Rose and Gramps already here, the safest place for them was under his roof. And that made him open his Bible, which made him realize how needy they all were.

Still, something inside him had shifted. At the accident scene, holding her had driven home how shaken she was. In the kitchen, watching her go through ordinary motions after extraordinary fear, he'd realized how much she carried on her shoulders. Abby might be a former officer of the law, but she was also a single mother who was desperate to keep her child safe. And for William, that was enough to stir an ache of responsibility he couldn't ignore.

Abby's chest lifted with a deep breath. "Robert mentioned how much he disliked the retirement home. Could he have said something to the owner or staff that could have upset them?"

Her statement provided a much-needed bucket of cold water. He was supposed to be taking care of his grandfather, not swooning over a pretty face.

When William brought Gramps home, Uncle Joe had resisted, forcing Gramps to sign paperwork granting William power of attorney over medical and financial decisions. It was the only way to prevent Uncle Joe from sending Gramps back. But it hadn't stopped Uncle Joe from suggesting Gramps would be better off there under constant care. But that power of attorney granted William the final say, and he said Gramps should spend his final days in the place he called home.

Abby's exhalation fluffed the strands of hair that had fallen loose and framed her face. "When I spoke up at my last job, it ruffled some feathers. Maybe Gramps's comments poked the hornet's nest."

William sighed. "I looped in the police. They've looked into it. Nothing was out of sorts at the home."

She fingered the note. "Clearly, someone is upset that I'm still here helping Robert. Until we know why, we need to stay alert."

Abby's relaxed posture and easy breathing while she discussed their tormentor puzzled him. She seemed unbothered by the note. Abby was the opposite of Claire. Where Claire had been soft and quiet, Abby was sharp edges and assertive. Claire stayed home with Ella, wanting to be a full-time mother. Abby had a career she excelled in. They couldn't be more different.

Yet, both stirred something in him, and that unsettled him most of all. It was evidence that it was time to revert to the original plan. Abby and Carson needed to move to the cottage. Their relationship was supposed to be a business one. Professional and formal. Because he wasn't ready for more.

Claire died three years ago. Long enough, according to his friends, for him to date again. They'd tried fixing him up, but he wouldn't play along. When they invited him to dinner and slipped in another single guest, he'd felt trapped. Everyone thought he should move on. But how does a person move on from losing the life they thought they'd have?

But Abby needed him.

That jolted him. Was that what appealed to him?

After Claire died, he'd spent some time in therapy through his church. One of the things he learned about himself was that he gravitated toward relationships where he was the caretaker. He'd cared for his alcoholic father until Gramps stepped in when he was eleven. He cared for Claire, whom he had met at church shortly after she had moved to town. She'd known no one, and he quickly became her entire world. He cared for her throughout her cancer, and now he cared for Ella and Gramps.

His insides twisted at the idea that he was using Abby to serve his own need to be needed. Another reason she should move into the cottage where clear lines could be drawn. But the thought wouldn't quiet. What if their troubles weren't over? What if the men who planted the drugs wanted to punish Abby for interfering? What if he failed them all?

A darker fear took hold. What if he opened his heart again only to lose someone the way he'd lost Claire? He wasn't sure he'd survive another loss. And he'd bet the peach farm that whatever this was, it wasn't over.

He pressed his thumb hard against his wedding band as if the familiar circle of metal could anchor him. His job was to keep Abby and Carson safe, whether they wanted his protection or not.

Footsteps pounded down the hallway.

"William!" Uncle Joe burst into the room. "Gramps is gone!"

CHAPTER
SEVEN

Abby leaped to her feet. "What do you mean, gone?" The note fluttered to the ground.

William was already striding across the room.

"Gone means gone." Joe glared at her, and his nostrils flared.

Abby jerked her head back. What was Joe's problem? The way he looked at her. Anger radiated from him. Her muscles stiffened like they did back on her patrol days when she was constantly prepared to react to a sudden threat.

"What did you say to him?" William angled his body away from Joe as he strode by him, shooting dark glances his way. Abby didn't need to be a body language expert to discern that William didn't trust Joe. The question was, why?

Abby hurried to catch up with William. Her scalp prickled as she passed Joe. The sudden coldness that hit her core when their gazes connected set off alarms. Police officers called it a gut feeling, and she learned a long time ago to trust her gut.

William flung open the back door to an empty porch. Heaviness filled her stomach.

"I didn't say nothing." Joe rubbed the tip of his nose. Joe avoided eye contact with William, who'd pressed his lips flat.

"Robert wouldn't just leave," Abby said.

"You calling me a liar?" Red swept across Joe's cheeks, and he jabbed his finger at Abby.

A shiver swept down her spine. Not of fear. She could take Joe down in less than three seconds if he turned on her. It was a realization. Joe said something to Robert, all right. He just didn't want to admit it.

"We can discuss the what later. Right now, we need to find Gramps." William curled his arms over his head and walked in a slow circle. "Where would he go?"

"He got all huffy and stomped down the steps. He went around the side of the house. I thought he was coming in the front door. I waited a few minutes to give him some space, but I can't find him." The tendons in Joe's neck were engorged. He jammed his hands into his armpits, and his shoulders jacked up to his earlobes.

Joe's afraid. The realization hit with certainty. But of what? Of Robert getting hurt in his vulnerable state? Beads of sweat gathered on Joe's upper lip, and he swept the back of his hand across his forehead. If Abby had him in the interrogation room, she'd up the temperature to increase his discomfort. Isolated, Joe's outrage, physical response, and general mannerisms meant nothing. But combined, they raised her hackles.

"What about the cottage?" Abby suggested. "Would Robert go to the cottage?"

William pinched the bridge of his nose and squeezed his eyes tight. "He used to spend a lot of time there before Gram died. But since we started using it for guests, he's stayed away. Besides, we haven't reopened it since the break-in. He wouldn't go there knowing it was closed off."

It might be closed off, but Rose had told Abby it was ready. Abby had been waiting for William to announce it was time for her to return to the cottage. But last night came and went, and he'd said nothing at breakfast. The police would have released the scene days ago. The delay made little sense.

"Gramps spent time in the cottage?" Joe's eyes widened.

A bitter tang filled Abby's mouth. Did no one in Robert's family know him? How was it that William, who'd only been home less than a year, knew Robert better than Joe, who'd been managing everything prior to William's return?

"You check the cottage," William instructed his uncle. "Abby and I will walk the orchard."

The pit in Abby's gut grew larger and larger with each step they took away from the house. After stopping to tell Rose what was happening, and asking her to phone if she saw Robert, Abby followed William deep into the rows of peach trees. His breathing grew heavier and louder. A sheen of sweat covered his forehead as he slapped branches from his face.

"William."

He pushed between two trees, cutting between the rows the exact way he'd told her never to cut between the rows.

"William." She squeezed his arm.

He lifted a face carved with anguish and fear. She let her hand slip down into his. "We'll find him. He's here some-where. He couldn't have gone far."

The not yet ripe peaches had no smell, but their weight sagged the branches.

"Robert!" Abby cupped the fingers of one hand around her mouth and hollered.

William followed suit. "Gramps!"

There had to be over two thousand trees in the orchard. It would take hours to walk the rows. Time Robert might not have if his dementia had flared and he got hurt.

"I shouldn't have left him alone." But even as Abby spoke the words, she knew it was ridiculous to take ownership of what had happened. Gramps had been with his son. There was no reason for her to stay and babysit the men.

"Did you hear what Uncle Joe and Gramps were talking about?"

"Something about papers being signed. Gramps said Joe needed to speak with you. That's when I left. It seemed too personal for a staff member to listen in on."

William stopped. "You're more than staff."

Her breath bottled. Was she? The intensity of the last few weeks had forged a connection between them that defied logic. She hadn't been here that long. But in her soul, she felt like more than hired help. They'd welcomed her into their family. And it scared her.

Because every family she'd been part of had let her down.

She unbuttoned the top button of her shirt and fanned her warm face. She didn't have time to think about that. "Robert!"

A rustling sounded a few rows over. She turned toward the noise, momentarily freezing at the distinct sound of a cocking gun.

She threw herself at William. "Gun!"

They tumbled to the ground in a tangle of legs and arms. She was going to cover him, protect him from gunfire, but he turned the tables.

He flipped them and covered her with his body. He threw an arm over the back of his head and turtled.

Nothing.

No shots. No panic.

Her mouth dried up. A roar in her skull built in intensity. Her ears hummed. Tingling swept up her neck and across her cheeks. Had she been mistaken? No. A cop never forgot that sound. It didn't matter how long it had been since she'd carried a gun. She would always know the sound of one cocking, and her body would always react as they had trained her.

William's chest heaved. Each inhalation pressed his ribs against hers. His warm breath washed over her cheek. The weight of him spread from her toes to her head. Her pulse thudded hard, heat surging under her skin. Not embarrassment. Something more unsettling.

He lifted his head. Cautiously. Slowly.

Their eyes met. His mouth was inches from hers. His gaze flicked to her lips before snapping back to her eyes, as if he wasn't sure whether to lean closer. The edges of her vision fuzzed. William had tried to protect her. She couldn't remember the last time she'd felt like someone else was looking out for her. Like she was safe with them.

His head dropped a millimeter. If he dipped it just a millimeter more—

A faint moan came from their left.

She turned her head. From their position on the ground, she could see the feet of a prone body a few rows over. She shoved William aside and lurched to her feet.

"Robert!" She cut through the trees and dropped beside him on her knees. "Are you okay?"

He struggled to sit up, so she slipped her arm under him and helped him lean his back against the tree.

William appeared on Robert's other side.

"I must have fallen." Robert rubbed his head. When he pulled his hand back, the smear of red made him sway. "My head hurts."

Abby's chest constricted. Robert was bleeding, and she had been lying there hoping William might kiss her. Shame flared hot. *Focus.*

ABC. Airway, breathing, circulation.

Airway. Robert was talking. His voice sounded normal, albeit a bit strained from whatever had happened.

Breathing. Robert's chest moved rhythmically. But was it sufficient? He showed no increased work of breathing or lacerations on the trachea.

Circulation. Sweat glistened on his pale skin. He had no distended neck veins. "Did you lose consciousness?" Abby pressed two fingers against Robert's wrist. A fast but steady pulse throbbed against her touch.

"I'm not sure." Gramps squeezed his eyes as if he were trying to pull up a memory that refused to surface. "I wanted space. Joey was there."

Abby probed around the wound on Robert's head, watching him for a reaction to her touch. "I don't think it needs stitches. Just a cleaning. We need to stop the bleeding."

William stripped to his white undershirt and pressed his balled-up button-down in her hands. The simple act of him wordlessly handing over his shirt shouldn't affect her, but it did.

Abby ignored the low jolt in her stomach and pressed the fabric against the wound. "Can you keep pressure on this?" she asked William.

He took over trying to stem the flow of blood from Robert's scalp.

"Can you tell me what happened?" She continued to assess Robert, who was alert and voice responsive. Both good signs. "What's the next thing you remember?"

Would he mention the gunman? Did she imagine the sound of the cocking gun when it was actually Robert, a few rows over, that she'd heard?

Except every officer knew the sound of a gun.

She ran her hands gently down each of Robert's limbs, feeling for injuries, watching his expression as she applied pressure, looking for pain responsiveness. Thank the Lord he wasn't unresponsive.

"The next thing I remember was waking up to your pretty face."

She swallowed. Waking up implied he'd lost consciousness. Was this an accident? Or was Robert targeted because she failed to leave like the note instructed?

She forced her mind back on track. She wasn't a cop. Robert needed her to stay on task as a caregiver.

Exposure came next. Keeping the man's dignity in mind, Abby opened a few buttons on Robert's shirt to examine his chest. She turned his palms over and checked his hands. Hiked up his pant legs to examine his lower legs. She drew a breath through her nose and quietly exhaled. He was going to be okay.

William's gaze stuck to her like glue. He should watch his grandfather.

She gritted her teeth. "Come on, Robert. Let's get you back to the house."

"I told you to call me Gramps," he groused.

Her mouth softened. *Gramps* was going to be just fine.

She bit her lower lip to keep from smiling. "Okay, Gramps, let's go."

William slipped his arm under his grandfather and hoisted him to his feet. They sandwiched Robert and hobbled their way back to the main house. Abby scoured the trees the entire way. There was no evidence of another person. No reason for her to think they were in danger.

Except the feeling in her gut.

"I DON'T UNDERSTAND." William stroked his eyebrow, trying to rub away the early pains of a headache. "Explain it to me again."

Uncle Joe repositioned himself on the sofa. The couch sat lower than the armchair that William occupied. It wasn't until William made Gramps's home office his own that he realized his grandfather had sanded an inch off the feet of the sofa. Then Gramps had swapped out the original armchair feet for taller ones. It was a subtle, passive-aggressive tactic designed to give him the position of power. If it were any other day, he and Uncle Joe might have shared a laugh over it. But with Gramps at Urgent Care *again*, William would take whatever edge he could to even the playing field between him and the man he'd usurped. Once they were sure Gramps wasn't seriously injured, Abby took Gramps to the hospital. He and Uncle Joe had some things to discuss.

Uncle Joe's jerky movements and stiff jaw said more than his words, and Uncle Joe rarely minced his words. William grew up knowing exactly what his uncle thought about William's "deadbeat" dad.

"Gramps was just found bleeding, and you're worried about balancing the books?" Joe dragged a hand down his face. "You're in over your head. Just admit it." Joe never missed an opportunity to undermine William's decisions for the farm.

"We've been over this—"

"How the farm is my birthright and not yours?"

"I didn't ask Gramps to give me power of attorney."

"But you didn't turn it down either." Joe paused as if he heard how angry he sounded. He leaned forward, nodding as he spoke. "Let me help. I can manage the farm, and you take care of Gramps. I figured out the problem and was trying to fix things when he signed everything over to you."

If Uncle Joe knew what the issue was, maybe they could turn the ship around in time to save the farm.

"Dad got creative with the books," Joe said. "He'd move money from the farm's line of credit to make a minimum payment on a loan. Then he'd take the household money to pay the line of credit and buy his groceries on his credit card. It's a way of shifting funds around to make your minimum payments without actually making a payment. He did it all the time."

Except that didn't sound like the Gramps William knew.

Uncle Joe splayed his hands wide. "I get it. I managed the accounts when Gramps went into the home."

At the word home, all the softness inside William hardened. "Home is a generous description of that place you dumped your father."

Joe scowled. The tips of his ears reddened, and his leg bounced. "They have a good reputation in town."

Except Joe would have known if he had visited that Gramps was unhappy. William visited twice. The second time only to confirm that what he saw that first day wasn't a fluke. Gramps was horribly unhappy. William hadn't even finished asking Gramps if he wanted to return to the farm before Gramps started packing. And despite all his mental decline, Gramps wasn't as slow-witted as Joe claimed. Gramps had enough sense to call in his lawyer and draft the changes to his will so that Joe couldn't overrule William and send him back.

"If things keep going on the current trajectory, the farm will be broke by Christmas. That's what I was trying to tell Dad before he stormed off. He doesn't want to hear it, but it's time to revisit the idea of selling and using the profit to pay for long-term care for Dad."

William's heart twanged. Gramps knew his time on earth was short, and he'd been abundantly clear that his final wish was to live these days in the home he shared with Grams. "Shouldn't we honor his wishes to stay here?"

"He won't be able to stay here if the place goes into foreclosure. We need to get out while there is still a potential profit."

William drew a deep breath and held it. Picking a fight with Uncle Joe would not help Gramps. For a man to bypass both his sons and hand the family's legacy to his grandchild was no small thing. Gramps made William the executor. There was a reason Gramps chose him and not Joe.

And not William's father. Not that he could have chosen William's father. William hadn't heard from his dad in years. Pain scorched the back of William's throat. "Gramps built this place into what it is. It's his right to use that equity to pay for whatever life he wants now. He doesn't owe us a profit after his death."

Joe's left eye twitched, but he held his tongue.

"I'll think about what you said, Uncle Joe. I promise. But my priority is to honor Gramps's wishes."

"About those—"

"Don't—" William held up his palm.

"Don't what? Point out the obvious? A pretty face has besotted you, and you're not thinking about Gramps at all. You're thinking about her. She's muddied the water."

"Abby took your father to the doctor after cleaning his head wound and making sure he was okay. She's motivated Gramps more than anyone else. She makes him laugh. And she found him when he was lost today. Not me. Not you. She did."

"She's a problem, and you're too blind to see it." Uncle Joe folded his arms across his chest.

William tried to view things from Uncle Joe's point of view. Of course, Uncle Joe was angry. Gramps bypassed him and made William his heir and then gave no reason. He just said to read Luke 15:11-32.

William didn't need to look up the familiar reference to the story of the prodigal son. He figured his dad was the prodigal, and that left Joe as the elder brother. Uncle Joe was the one who stayed in town and worked the farm, growing more bitter and entitled with each passing day. William was convinced that the parable was not only about the son who left but also about the heart condition of the son who stayed. He just didn't know where he fit, as the grandson, into the story.

William never mentioned the Scripture reference to Uncle Joe. That was up to Gramps. Besides, Uncle Joe wasn't the bad guy here. He stayed, and he was grieving. They were all mourning the loss of the man Gramps once was. No one lived forever. And everyone lamented differently. "I hear you, Uncle Joe. I do. Leave it with me a bit longer. I'm still praying about it."

A rap on the door interrupted whatever Joe might have said in reply.

"Come in."

Abby stepped into the room and pulled the door closed behind her. Her gaze bounced between William and Joe. "The doctor said Robert is fine. I've settled him upstairs and will check on him regularly. I thought you'd like to know."

"Thank you for taking such good care of him. We're grateful for your kindness to Gramps."

Uncle Joe covered a snort with a cough.

Abby and Joe locked eyes. She held his glare with such force and authority that William straightened in his chair and adjusted his collar.

"Do you have a problem with me?" she asked Uncle Joe. "I get the feeling you do."

Direct and to the point.

Uncle Joe shifted. He tried to cross an ankle over a knee but fumbled like he couldn't figure out exactly why he was so uncomfortable on the couch. Joe huffed, giving up on trying to appear unruffled. "I guess I do. I mean, things were pretty quiet around here until you showed up."

The declaration hung between them, and Abby blinked first, pulling back as if slapped. She recovered quickly, rearranging her features into a neutral expression. If it weren't for the tiny pulse throbbing in her collarbone, William might have thought the comment slid right off her. "Are you implying Gramps's injuries are my fault?"

Joe launched to his feet. "Dad felt unwell. Under the weather. She arrives," he points his finger at Abby, "and brings a drug cartel with her. She's attacked in his hospital room, and you don't see the connection?"

William inserted himself between Uncle Joe and Abby.

"Abby isn't the reason Gramps took off today. That's on you. You're the one who got him all riled up talking about paperwork." William drew attention away from Abby. "You don't have to like the decisions Gramps makes, but you need to respect them."

Abby fisted her hands on her hips. "Our bickering will not help Gramps."

"Don't call him that," Uncle Joe roared. "You are not part of this family." Uncle Joe flung open the office door and stomped out. The picture frames in the hallway rattled with the pounding of his feet. A few seconds later, the front door slammed.

Abby froze, her face ashen.

William burned with an ache to comfort Abby and assure her that Joe had no idea what he was talking about. Unless Uncle Joe had a point. Had his feelings for Abby muddied the water?

William scrubbed a hand down his face. Joe was right about one thing. Abby meant more to him than he was ready to admit. "The cottage is ready. You can move into it anytime."

Abby shifted. Was that regret? Sadness? He couldn't get a read on her. Her neck bent forward, and she allowed a wall of hair to swing down and conceal her face. By the time she lifted her head, a smile replaced her tense lips, and her watery eyes had dried. "Wonderful. You are probably eager to get your house back to yourselves."

William's expression felt tight and fake. He wasn't eager. Not really. But he needed some distance between them. Not for his sake, but for hers. The last thing Abby needed was attention from a man that wasn't genuine, and until he got a handle on his motives regarding his attraction to her, they needed space.

"I'll have a company move the rest of your belongings from the barn into the cottage for you." When her things were delivered the day after she arrived, they had temporarily placed them in the barn. She'd need them back now.

"Sounds good." Her smile failed to reach her eyes. "I'll go gather my things. Carson and I might as well move in tonight."

CHAPTER

EIGHT

Abby thrashed her legs and shot upright. The bedsheets twisted around her feet, and a faint sheen of sweat covered her body. She shivered. The hair on her nape and arms lifted. Another nightmare.

They'd come regularly since the accident. Sometimes she woke before they ditched the car. Other times, she saw the horror-stricken faces of the children. Tonight, the car caught fire. But instead of William in the seat beside her, it was Carson. And she couldn't free him.

Her muscles cramped. She should get up. Experience had proven it was better to rise, clear her head, and think about other things before trying to fall back to sleep, otherwise the dream would pick up where it left off, and she'd be back in that burning vehicle screaming Carson's name.

A backhand across her brow smeared dampness into her hairline. Battling midnight blazes wasn't a new phenomenon. She squinted at the alarm clock on the bedside table that failed to glow. The power must be out. That explained the heat. The ceiling fans couldn't circulate the air. She groped the bedside table for her phone. Nearly midnight.

Abby swallowed rawness. Water would help. She fisted her stinging eyes and shook her head. Everything seemed foggy. Off.

A steady crackle and hiss played in the background like an instrumental soundtrack to her dream. Her olfactory system misfired and was transmitting the wrong information to her brain, which was convinced a faint smell of smoke hung in her room. Funny how the elements of her dream lingered. She stuffed her feet into her slippers and staggered to the bedroom door. The crackling increased. The cottage had been quiet when she'd tucked Carson into bed. Exhausted, she'd fallen into her bed only an hour later.

Still rubbing her eyes, she reached for the doorknob, not registering its warmth until it was too late. The fumes hit first, then smoke. She gagged, staggered, and stumbled back. She slammed the door and pressed herself against the wall.

There's a fire.

Her pulse throbbed in her neck. *Carson!* Had she closed his bedroom door? The cottage only had two bedrooms, and Carson's was on the other side of the bathroom. Her bedroom had a connecting door that opened directly into the bathroom. She bolted to the bathroom and started the shower, throwing in the towel she'd hung to dry earlier.

Sometimes, in a new place, she left Carson's bedroom open so she'd hear him better if he called. Panic squeezed her chest. His room was closer to the fire. If his door was open, he'd be—

She gagged. More people died from smoke inhalation or from the fumes of the burning chemicals than they did from the actual flames.

She squeezed her eyes shut. If she'd left his door open, she would have left her door open as well.

Please, Lord.

Abby dumped her thick bathrobe into the shower, dousing it as well. Creaks and groans intensified in the house. Seconds. She had only seconds. She stepped into the stream of water and pulled the wet robe over her clothes, cinching it at the waist. She covered her head with the towel.

The bathroom's main door opened into the hallway, and it was closer to Carson's room. She stood in front of it, her body straining. The volume of the crackling soundtrack increased. *Help me, Lord.*

Wrapping her hand with the cuff of her robe, she tested the temperature of the doorknob. Warm but not burning. Covering her mouth and nose with the end of the towel, she sucked in a breath and flung open the door.

Fumes assaulted her. She crushed her eyes into slits. They immediately burned. An acrid scent scorched the back of her throat, and a hazy fog curled at the ceiling. She stooped to gulp cleaner air. A glow came from around the corner, but the flames hadn't reached the hallway yet. A pop of glass sounded, then something crashed.

Curling her elbow over her mouth, she coughed. Bitterness burned in her nostrils.

Her throat spasmed, throwing her into dry heaves. She pressed her fists to the sides of her head, straining to see through the gray. Only gray. No orange, red, or yellow. The gray thickened like swirling molasses.

She had seconds.

With each inhalation, she fought the impulse to retch. She rubbed the now-warm towel against her eyes. The press of suffocating cotton over her mouth made her gag. Still blurry. Popping and cracking increased like popping corn in the fire. The constant crinkling of paper. A sound ingrained in her brain. A sound she could never forget.

Not now. Focus.

Keeping her hands under her robe, she turned Carson's doorknob. Her legs momentarily weakened. She shoved in, yanking it shut behind her. She took the towel from her head and stuffed it into the gap under the door.

A shiver zipped down her back. A shiver while the heat skyrocketed. She stumbled toward the bed. "Carson, Carson! Wake up, baby. We have to go outside."

Had her parents woken up? Did they try to escape? Were they afraid for her, consumed with the same terror that filled her? All the questions that she'd never allowed to land now hit with full force, stealing what little breath that remained. Had her parents stumbled through smoke-filled hallways, calling her name, unaware she'd broken curfew? Did they refuse to leave the house without her? Was it her fault they were dead?

Her vision tunneled. She couldn't. Not this. Not now. Because she knew. She wasn't leaving this house without her child.

Her knees thudded against the floor by the bed. She was too hot. Carson's chest rose and fell in a steady rhythm. She shook him. "Carson!"

He'd never been easy to wake. She didn't wait. She gathered him into her arms and stood, the dead weight slowing her down. For one frozen second, she didn't know what to do. Her eyes flicked around the room. The door. The closet. The window.

Another crash vibrated the floor. The cottage screamed in agony. The groaning of compromised beams and household chemicals exploding filled her head until she couldn't distinguish between the past and the present. She couldn't think. Couldn't breathe.

She lurched toward the window, knocking over the bedside table. The lamp clattered to the floor. Its shade popped off, and the bulb shattered. The cottage was a single-level structure. The drop wouldn't be too bad.

She fumbled with the window. She couldn't open it. Not while holding Carson. But letting go was not an option. She tightened her grip for an impossible second. Her heartbeat thrashed in her ears. Logic fought panic. She had to put him down. She wedged him between the front of her legs and the wall, needing to feel him. "Carson!" She ran her fingertips along the window seams. "Mommy needs you to wake up. I need you to help me."

He stirred against her legs, and her knees nearly buckled. "I'm hot."

She fumbled with the lock, and she finally slid the window up. Coolness rushed through the window screen and brushed her face. She wept. The back of the cottage remained free of flames. "I know, baby. We are going outside. It's cooler outside."

She dropped to her knees. A sob rocketed through her. She shook his drowsy body. "Baby, wake up. We have to get out of here."

His lids fluttered and fully opened. His gaze leaped from confusion to panic in a single blink. "Mommy?"

"We have to get out the window."

Carson wrapped his arms around her legs and buried his face in her shins.

Her parents had thought she was home. They must have

tried to get to her room. That was why they died. That was why they never escaped.

Smoke trickled in under the door and around the towel. She couldn't find the release on the screen. She fumbled along the four edges. The taut webbing refused to budge. She grabbed the fallen lamp and hurled it at the screen. A warrior cry shredded her lungs as the lamp bounced back.

Carson jolted against her.

She retrieved the lamp. The broken bulb was still screwed in. Using the ragged edge of the glass, she slashed the screen.

She couldn't think about her parents right now. Only Carson mattered.

The mesh ripped. She tossed the lamp and peeled back the screen. "Now, Carson."

He coughed, tightening his grip on her. The towel under the door wasn't sufficient to completely block the smoke, but the toxins worried her more. They'd kill them first. Modern houses were filled with materials that became toxic when burned.

She couldn't lose Carson. Not like this. Not ever.

"I'm going to help you outside."

"No!" He rubbed his face back and forth on her legs and tightened his hold. "No, Mommy!"

She peeled him off her. "Stop!"

He clawed wildly, trying to crawl over her shoulder and away from the window. It was dark outside. She couldn't see the ground, but she knew it was there, close enough that the drop wouldn't hurt them, far enough that Carson refused to let go.

She shoved him over the windowsill and through the screen.

"Mommy!" He twisted and scrambled for a hold on the

edge, his voice shrill. But he had to drop. She had to get him out of the house. She steeled herself against the wild panic in his eyes. Betrayal. Not understanding. She'd have to pry his fingers from the ledge.

Another crash sounded behind her.

She tugged his hands free. A primal wail ripped from him. His nails raked down her wrist as she let him go with a sob.

Her baby.

He screamed.

Hissing filled her ears.

"Run to William. Get William." She heaved a leg over the windowsill.

Carson curled into a lump on the ground. She couldn't make out any details because she could only see his shadowy form.

"Now!" The shrillness of her command jerked him.

He stood. Flickering light illuminated his face. The fire must be creeping around the back. Tears streaked his cheeks. Eyes overly bright. Staring but not seeing.

She coughed, her body slipping over the edge. "Run, Carson!"

He backed away in quick, jerky steps before spinning toward the house. Lit only by the glow of the moon, the path from the cottage to the main house was dark, but thankfully, the porch lights were a steady beacon. That should be enough to guide him.

"Don't stop," she screamed. "I'm right behind you."

Interior lights in the row of cabins flicked on. Help was coming.

Her bare feet landed with a thud on the damp grass. She

refused to look back. She twisted and rolled her ankle. Her legs collapsed.

Blades of grass stroked her cheek. The coolness of the earth a welcome contrast to her hot lungs. She pushed herself up onto her hands and knees. She had to get away. She crawled, relief over their escape making her giddy. They were safe. Out. The flames couldn't take them.

But the truth warred with her memory.

The emptiness between the cottage and the house devoured Carson, but it couldn't swallow his howls.

SCREAMING JOLTED William from his sleep, followed by pounding on the front door. The dog whined in the hallway. Then, a panicked scream trickled through the fogginess in his brain.

William threw off the bedcovers. That's when he heard the roar. A roar that turned his insides out. It was a sound like none he'd ever heard before. William flew down the stairs, and Dreyfuss stuck to his heel. He flung the front door open, and Carson fell inside, screaming. "Help Mommy!"

Tears streaked Carson's face. His chest heaved. Wild panic filled his eyes, but he was unhurt. Relief slammed through William.

"Rose!" William bellowed. "Go to Rose." He pointed Carson toward her bedroom.

William was already across the porch and down the stairs, not waiting to see if Carson had obeyed when every-thing stopped. The cottage lit the night sky with a hellish glow. Murky smoke swirled. Flames licked the windows like the blazing tongue of the devil.

He couldn't breathe. Couldn't think. Couldn't move. He staggered against the stair railing.

"I called 911," Rose shouted from behind, jolting him from his stupor. She pressed Carson into her legs where he had buried his face, but positioned herself so he was as far from the door as possible, as if that bit of extra distance might protect him.

Carson sobbed.

"Carson, where's your mom?"

"My room," he hiccuped. He pressed his face further into Rose's legs, and she swayed, making quiet shushing sounds.

William bounded across the lawn. The damp grass soaked the hem of his pajama bottoms. Questions peppered his mind, but all he could do was chant. *No, Lord. No. Don't take her too. Don't.* He should never have sent her back to the cottage. He should have insisted she stay in the main house.

The heat from the blaze hit him first. The front was fully engulfed, but the bedroom windows were around the back. He sprinted around the corner of the house.

Help me, Lord. Help me find her in time. Help me save her.

The back of the cottage was not as engaged as the front. Smoke billowed out the windows, but the only flames burned at the corners. The screen from Carson's bedroom window flapped. There was no sign of Abby.

He spun, searching the darkness. "Abby!"

"Is everybody out?" Jethro panted. "I don't see anyone." The wail of sirens grew in intensity. Headlights lit the dirt path leading off the main road. Probably a neighbor coming to see if they needed help.

The beam from the vehicle illuminated a silhouette. It hobbled toward him, and without overthinking it, William crushed Abby in his arms. "Yes, everybody's out."

Jethro sagged. "Everybody's out," he shouted to the workers gathering at the back of the cottage. The blaze had roused everybody.

"Carson? Where's Carson?" Abby's breaths rasped and tremors rocked her frame.

"Carson's okay. He's at the house with Rose."

She crumpled. William supported her full weight, welcoming the feel of her in his arms. He tenderly moved her further from the thickening smoke, turning their backs to the blaze. It wouldn't do either of them any good to watch it burn. He tightened his hold on her.

"I couldn't find him in the dark." Abby babbled into his shoulder. Her damp robe and wet hair seeped through his thin pajama top.

William pressed his cheek against the top of her head. "Carson's safe. He came to the house. Rose has him. He's safe." He kept repeating it, and he'd continue until she finally heard him.

But was he really safe? They'd returned the drugs. Whoever had targeted Carson and Abby should have backed off. Was the fire a crazy coincidence?

William didn't believe in coincidences.

Headlights from the approaching vehicle lit them up. His neighbor, Henry, leaped from the driver's seat. "Is everyone okay? We saw the blaze from the house."

Fire trucks screamed into the driveway.

"Everyone is safe." William assured his neighbor.

"Jethro, would you mind going to the house and telling Rose that Abby is with me? Carson is with Rose."

"You bet." Jethro hurried across the lawn.

William moved Abby further from the blaze. Fire trucks

rolled in, and the men moved as a machine, unrolling hoses, examining the perimeter, doing what firefighters did.

Another vehicle rolled in. William recognized Isabelle Barlow from town. She worked at the paper.

"I want to see Carson." Abby's chest heaved, and she pulled back and hugged herself, rocking gently.

Of course, she did. "I'll take you."

William touched base with the fire chief, who said he'd come to the house to speak with them once the blaze was under control. The paramedics would look everyone over at the house.

William slung his arm around Abby's shoulders and steered her away from the cottage, where flames continued to consume the shingles and siding. She didn't need him to hold her any longer. She'd pulled herself together. But he needed to hold her. He needed to feel her warm skin and know she was safe.

They weren't even on the porch before Gramps flung open the front door. "Is everyone all right?"

"We're fine, Gramps. Just shook up."

Carson pushed past Gramps and hurled himself at his mother.

She crouched, rocking back from his momentum and absorbing the hit.

"I was scared."

"Me too, buddy. Me too." She pressed her nose into the crook of his neck and shoulder and inhaled. She lifted Carson, balancing him on her hip, looking him over. "Are you good? No scratches or owies?"

He extended his arms, looking them over. He pointed to a scratch on his forearm. "Owie here."

She pressed her lips to it. "That must be from the window."

William winced. He could only imagine their panicked escape and what it took for Abby to get Carson out of the house.

Rose draped a thick blanket over Abby's shoulders. "You're soaked through. I'll make some coffee. I still have some of Carson's play clothes here. I'll get him changed. He wouldn't let me before."

Carson burrowed further into Abby.

Abby's lips brushed Carson's ear. "I'm okay, Carson. You helped me by getting William. You did good. I'm proud of you."

He snuggled in.

"Mommy is getting you all wet." She set Carson on his feet. "Can you put on some dry clothes?"

He nodded, and he slipped his hand into Rose's. Everything was right with the world now that his mother was here.

Abby shivered, and William realized she didn't even have dry clothes to change into. They'd moved all her belongings back to the cottage. Everything except what was still in the barn. A sense of helplessness overwhelmed him. Hadn't Abby been through enough? Why this, too?

"I'll get a thick sweatshirt and sweatpants you can change into." He hurried to his room, returning with a gray hoodie and sweatpants. "They have a drawstring. They won't be perfect, but they're dry."

"Thank you." Abby slipped into the restroom to change.

William watched her go. Was this connected to Abby and the drugs? What if it was connected to the things happening to Gramps? What if William brought this danger to Abby and

Carson? What if it was his fault? What if he couldn't keep them safe?

Gramps's hand landed heavily on William's shoulder. "It's not your fault."

"I never said it was."

"I might be old, but I ain't stupid." Gramps gave his shoulder a squeeze before releasing it. "I've been taking care of you long enough to know how you think." Gramps waited until William turned to meet his gaze. "This is not your fault," Gramps repeated. "You can't put the people you love in a bubble."

"Love?" William's ears heated.

Gramps scoffed. "You think I don't have eyes? You look at her the way you used to look at Claire. The way I looked at my sweet Ruth. You're falling for her. You're just not ready to see it yet."

Oh, he saw it all right. He just fought it. Abby was here for Gramps. That was it. "Maybe you're confusing my sense of responsibility with love."

There was something about Gramps's indulgent smile that made him feel placated. "You took care of your dad, then Claire, and now me. You're a good man, William. Better than most."

If that were true, why did it feel like God was punishing him? Why did he lose everyone he loved? He swallowed, but the lump in his throat failed to move. He was in biblical counseling long enough to know that thought was flat out wrong. God did not work that way. But right theology didn't always touch those deep places where it hurt. Not in the moment. Not when he was still reeling from the potential loss and fear still wrapped its bony fingers around his throat and squeezed.

Abby padded down the hallway, her bare feet slapping on the floor. A wave of incompetence washed over him. She didn't even have shoes. He turned to promise that he'd get her everything she needed tomorrow, but the words died before he could speak.

She'd rolled the cuffs of his gray sweats, exposing a bit of ankle. The sleeves bunched on her forearm. She'd braided her wet hair. A faint blush tainted her cheeks. "I left the wet clothes in the tub."

There was something incredibly intimate about this moment. Something he couldn't have anticipated and was powerless to resist. His heart shifted, and Gramps snickered. "You're right. You're not falling. Not one little bit."

Hours later, after the fire had been extinguished, and the medics had examined Abby and Carson, the chief kept his word. He rapped his knuckles on the front door.

William opened the door. "Let me grab Abby."

He found her in the back room speaking with Isabelle. Their heads were close together, and as Abby spoke, Isabelle furiously took notes. A momentary lapse of judgment caused him to pause and listen. He heard his name, caught odd words like history, father, and crime. Then, the pinch of the Holy Spirit caused him to pull back. Stealing information that wasn't his to hear wasn't much different from other kinds of theft. And eavesdropping never turned out well for the listener.

Exhaustion pulled at William, but he resisted. He faked a cough, and the women hushed. "The fire chief is here."

"Thanks," Abby said. Was it his imagination, or was her smile tight?

The group gathered around the kitchen table. William knew what the chief was going to say. "Arson, right?"

"Probably." The chief's lips pressed into a tight line. "Why is that your first guess?"

William kept one eye on Abby as he brought the chief up to date on the recent events. Isabelle wrote more in her notepad.

Abby pushed herself to her feet. Wrapping her arms around her body, she stared out the window toward the cottage. The sun had crested the curve of the earth and cast new morning mercies over the land.

"I'll get one of my guys to give you the names of a few restoration and clean-up companies, but don't do anything until I give you the go-ahead." The chief's gaze followed Abby's movements. "If we confirm it's arson, it will delay the insurance payout."

William nodded. "I understand. They'll need to investigate." He had nothing to hide. They could poke into his life all they wanted.

"Once you're cleared, things will speed up."

Abby's head snapped their way. "Once he's cleared? You think he had something to do with this?"

"Personally? No, but statistically, most arson cases are traced back to the owner looking for a payout. They have a process they need to work through."

She could not hide her shock and disgust at the suggestion. An unexpected release of tension swept through William. She didn't believe he was involved. Not for a second.

His eyes closed as relief sank in.

CHAPTER
NINE

Abby might not know how she felt about her and Carson's return to the main house, but Carson wasn't as indecisive. He fell back into his old routine with the ease and flexibility that accompanied childhood. The trauma from the fire didn't seem to faze him. At least not during the daytime hours. They shared a bed the first few nights. He tossed and turned enough that she expected nightmares to wake him, but he'd slept through.

The nightmares belonged to her.

Abby placed a bowl on the kitchen table in front of Carson and absentmindedly poured a sugary cereal into it. After adding milk and handing him a spoon, she grabbed herself a coffee. "I'm going to sit on the porch." Carson was a ridiculously slow eater, and he was used to finishing breakfast alone while Abby got ready for work.

She wandered onto the porch. She had asked Isabelle to dig into the Roth family and who might have a beef against them while she used her position to try to learn what she could on her end. Despite having no proof except her gut, Isabelle assured her that the instinct of a former law enforcement officer was enough for her. It had only been a week, but Isabelle had learned something. She was calling this morning.

Abby closed the front door behind her and settled onto the porch swing. Involving Isabelle was the right thing to do. The police weren't about to share the details of their investigation with Abby. She got that. But they had to get to the bottom of this before someone got hurt. If that was true, why did she feel like such a traitor? Her phone rang, saving her from thinking too deeply.

"I haven't got long." Isabelle cut right to it. "The Roth family has lived in the community for generations. In the last twenty years, they've made positive contributions to the community."

Abby's ears perked at the specific mention of a timeline. "What about prior to those twenty years? Did something happen twenty years ago?"

Isabelle inhaled noisily. "It's all rumor, you know. I found nothing I could use. I'm still digging."

Abby's middle tightened. "Please. I need to know. For Carson."

"William's grandfather was suspected of cooking the books. It might have been for organized crime, which has a strong presence in Niagara. It might have been for personal gain. There was suspicion, but nothing could ever be proven."

Sweet Robert laundering money? It didn't ring true. "If Robert was cooking the books, when did he stop?"

"When he gained custody of William."

William had told her Robert had raised him, but she

didn't know why. He never offered the information, and she felt uncomfortable prying.

"William's dad was a closet alcoholic," Isabelle continued. "It got worse when William's mom got sick. After she passed, his grandfather stepped in and gave his son an ultimatum. William's dad chose the drink."

Abby's heart lurched. She knew what it was to have people you love fail to prioritize you. "Could you trace any of the recent trouble to William's dad?"

Isabelle hesitated. "Not yet. I found his contact information. Would you like it?"

"Yes, please."

Abby's phone dinged. "I just sent it to you. Look, I've gotta go. Can we meet tomorrow at the paper?"

"Sure." That would give Abby enough time to reach out to William's dad and learn if he had a hand in what was going on.

They disconnected, and Abby tried William's father before she lost her nerve. She got his voicemail, so she left a message, introducing herself as a former police officer and asking him to return her call. She had some questions about his father and how he ran the orchard, and questions about his son.

Abby returned to the kitchen just as Ella wandered in.

Ella rubbed a fist into her bleary eyes, staggering like a fawn just finding its legs. It was impossible to feel anything but love for this sweet girl.

"Good morning, Ella."

Rose trailed Ella and went right for the coffee. She smiled a greeting to Abby.

Her heart quickened. If Ella was up, so was William. She could envision him sitting in the large chair in his office or maybe on the back porch, enjoying the morning. Would he have heard her conversation with Isabelle?

Ella's eyes brightened at Abby's greeting, and she rushed over to wrap her arms around her legs.

Abby's hand dropped lightly onto Ella's head. She ran her fingers through her silky hair. With her in a borrowed bathrobe nursing a coffee and fond thoughts of William and the kids in their jammies, it all felt so normal. Like they were a family. Except family didn't secretly investigate one another.

Carson's sleepiness evaporated at the sight of his friend. Ella skipped to Carson. She whispered something in his ear, giggling the entire time. He stuffed in another mouthful of cereal as he leaned closer to her, cocking his head. Milk dribbled from the corner of his lips. He nodded along with whatever she said.

Ella finished, clasped her hands under her chin, and tipped her head back to look up at Abby. Her eyelids fluttered as she blinked rapidly. "Can we play?"

Carson's rhythmic motion of shoveling cereal into his mouth paused.

Abby exchanged a glance with Rose, who nodded. After all they've been through, a little indulgence wouldn't hurt.

"I'll feed him some more later when Ella eats breakfast," Rose promised.

Abby leaned her hip against the table and gave him an indulgent smile. "You can play for a bit, then you have to eat the rest of your breakfast."

"Yay!" Carson shoved back his chair, and the children skipped off together, hand in hand, like siblings.

Abby took another sip of coffee, her gaze trailing Rose as she followed the children. There was a time she thought she'd have a big family, that after she married and started having babies, she'd have one after another until a half dozen tugged on her apron. But Carson arrived much sooner than she'd planned.

Or more accurately, because she failed to plan.

She pressed a cool palm to her hot cheek. She'd had too much to drink, celebrating the closure of a tough case. That was her first poor decision. Crashing on a friend's couch for the night was the second poor decision. Her parents had been gone for years by that time, so there was no one to check on her, no one waiting for her to arrive home safely. No one reminding her to live according to the Word of God.

Her thoughtless choices snowballed, and nine months later, Carson appeared, and her life had never been the same. His arrival put her back on the straight and narrow path. Nothing sobered a self-focused young adult like becoming instantly responsible for the life and well-being of another human being. She regretted her lapse in moral judgment, and repented of her sin against God, but she never regretted Carson. He was a gift.

She was now a single mom. She might never marry and have that large family she once dreamed of, but God used it all for her good, and Lord willing, Carson's good. Who knew how long and how far she would have allowed the grief over losing her parents to push her from the Lord had God not permitted the natural consequences of the seeds she sowed?

She dumped the contents of Carson's now soggy cereal into the garbage and wiped droplets of milk off the table. Spending time in this home was changing her. She rarely lingered in deep theological thought, but it was impossible not to gravitate there when reminders of God and His sovereignty were all over the house. From the bronzed map on the office wall engraved with Psalm 24:1 to the kitchen sign inviting guests to 'taste and see the Lord is good', every place she set her eyes redirected her back to God.

She felt a gentle correction in her spirit. God was supposed to be central. But ever since Carson's birth, every decision revolved around Carson. It's why she left policing. When a friend reported her pregnancy against her wishes, Austin gave her the rundown of what would follow. She'd be put on light duty until after the baby was born because of the dangers of the job. That's when it hit her. Her child would never have a secure childhood if she worked as a police officer. He'd grow up afraid that she wouldn't come home from work. She couldn't do that to him. She wouldn't take the chance of leaving Carson an orphan.

Abby tossed the dishrag in the sink and pulled out the kitchen chair. She wrapped both her hands around her mug and leaned forward so the steam warmed her face. Carson was important and deserving of her best mothering, but he was not supposed to be the center of her world. She'd elevated her son to a place reserved for God, and she never would have realized it before coming here. Carson needed her to keep the right priorities because when parents messed up their priorities, it messed up the kids. She'd seen it a thousand times in her short police career.

Like when she and Austin were called to a domestic situation. In the end, the kids were removed from the home. She could still hear the mother wailing and the father cursing them. That call could have gone wrong a million different ways. Statistically, it could have become violent. No one responded well to their children being taken away, and not always because of love. Often, entitlement and defiance refused to yield to authority. No one was going to tell them what they could and couldn't do with their kids.

She decided that her baby would come first. He had to. But with a similar resolution, she decided now that Carson had to be second. God would come first.

But she wasn't 100 percent sure what that meant or how it should look. Carson's father wasn't around to weigh in back then, and he wasn't here now. He'd traipsed off to the coast to the job of his dreams, leaving her to carry Carson to term and make all the decisions.

She gazed out the window. How much easier would parenting be as a team? It was how God designed it. She felt like a peach tree bent under the weight of the fruit. Life was supposed to be different here. Simpler. Easier. But trouble followed them. It wasn't fair. It wasn't supposed to be this hard.

"Can we talk?" William startled her. She sloshed coffee over the rim of her mug. He grabbed the dishcloth from the sink and wiped the spill. "Rose and the kids are in the playroom, and Gramps is still sleeping."

"Sure." Sucking in a breath, her stomach hardened. He was going to ask her to leave. She steeled herself against the blow. It didn't matter. She hadn't been here long enough to put down roots or anything. She'd brought trouble to his house, and he had to protect Ella. She got it, but it still—

"I'm sorry," William said.

"We can be gone by dinner," she spoke at the same time he did.

"Wait, what?"

"Why are you sorry?" She tucked her hands under her thighs to stop fidgeting.

William's chest lifted with a deep inhalation. "The Fire

Chief called and confirmed the cottage fire was arson. It's my cottage. I asked you to leave the main house and move back into it. I said it was safe." His eyes softened. "I'm so sorry." He stretched his hand across the table but stopped shy of taking hers. His forehead wrinkled.

It was funny. In the emotionally charged moments they've shared, neither of them hesitated to reach for the other. But when things were safe, uncertainty returned. What were the boundaries of their relationship? It was more than employee and employer. After all they'd been through, it had to be. She covered his hands with hers. If he needed comfort, reassurance, well, it was the least she could do. "You have nothing to apologize for. The trouble followed me here. I brought this to you. Maybe if Carson and I leave, you and Ella will be safe."

William stared at where their hands connected. He turned her palms over and ran his thumb across the webbing between her thumb and index finger. Tiny shivers rippled down her spine. "What if it's more than that? Gramps has been saying for weeks someone was out to get him." William let go and hung his head. "I thought he was just being Gramps. Conspiracy theories and all."

"Do you think there is something to Robert's concerns?"

"I think we are trying to fit all the puzzle pieces into one picture. But what if there are two different puzzles?"

She sat back and cupped her elbow. Her fingertips skimmed along her jawline. Was it possible this wasn't connected to the drugs? Gramps was already unwell before she arrived. What if his head injury wasn't just a stumble outside? What if he really was in danger? She plucked at her bottom lip.

"William, I don't blame you for the fire. The blame rests

on the person who started it. Probably the man who planted the drugs on Carson. I've never blamed you."

"Did I hear you on the phone with Isabelle?"

Abby stiffened. How much could he have understood from her side of the conversation? And worse, did he hear her leave a message for his father? She cleared her throat. "Yes, Isabelle is following up after the fire." It was true. It just wasn't the whole truth.

"You know you can ask me anything, right?"

She shifted uncomfortably in her seat. She did. But she wasn't ready yet. She wanted to speak with his father and with a few more of the migrant workers first. "I do."

When she didn't follow up with a question, the silence grew uncomfortable. She felt like she'd let him down. She gently touched his shoulder.

The agony she read in his eyes nearly broke her. That was why they connected. That was why they fit so perfectly.

He was just as damaged as she was.

Uncle Joe studied the papers that William had spread out on the desk. In painful slow motion, Joe flipped them one by one, transferring them into a neat stack.

William's trepidation rose. After another restless night, he'd asked Uncle Joe to come and look at the Orchard's finances. William's ribs squeezed every time the corners of Uncle Joe's lips turned down. All this time, William had insisted that he could handle the fruit farm and Gramps on his own, but the evidence in front of them was indisputable. The farm was failing, and for Gramps's sake, William needed to set aside his pride and accept help. He would muster up the strength to do whatever it took to ensure Gramps had what he needed to make his final years on earth comfortable, even if it meant yielding to Uncle Joe.

Uncle Joe sighed and flipped another page.

The investigation into the cottage fire would delay the insurance payout. The fragile dam that William built around Gramps and their life together bowed under pressure. William rubbed his face. The scruff of his bristly chin scratched his palm. If only he could erase the last few days— no, that wasn't quite right. He wouldn't erase everything.

William was suddenly very aware of his heartbeat. He didn't regret the warmth of holding Abby in his arms or the surge of protectiveness that shot through him when she and Carson needed him. But William lifted his chin, and his expanded chest deflated. As much as he cared about them— cared about her—she couldn't stay. Not if it put them in the center of whoever had targeted the farm. Abby's argument that the trouble followed her to the farm was weakening. The drugs planted on Carson could have been an isolated incident, connected to the man the officer had patted down in the parking lot on the night she'd arrived. She'd merely been an easy target. The attacker at the hospital had focused on Gramps. Abby was just in the way. The threatening notes addressed to Abby could be from someone trying to get closer to Gramps. But why would someone fixate on a forgetful old man? William tapped a fist to his lips. Unless Abby was right, and sending her away increased the danger because she'd be facing it alone. His fingernails bit into his palms. Why wasn't life simpler?

"When will the insurance pay?" Joe bent over the numbers.

"After they close the investigation."

The muscles in Joe's neck corded, and he swore under his

breath. William's gaze darted to the doorway, wincing at the vulgarity. Those weren't words he wanted Ella picking up.

Joe sighed heavily. "This'll be tied up for months. The fire chief said they found the butt of a cigar near the point of origin, the same brand that Gramps used to smoke."

William stiffened. "That doesn't make sense. Gramps hasn't smoked in years." But he still had a carton of them in his closet. William saw them a while back when he was helping him move his things back in.

Was it only four months ago that William stormed the doors of the retirement home and busted Gramps out? Gramps had whooped like a cowboy in those old western movies he liked. He called it a jailbreak. The memory made the tightness in William's face soften. They never looked back.

Until today.

William cradled his head. What had he done? If Gramps had become confused, could he have forgotten he'd quit smoking? An improperly extinguished cigar could have started the fire. "Do you really think it could have been Gramps?"

"What's the alternative?"

William shrugged. He wasn't ready to tell Joe everything.

Joe stared at him. "Did you know this isn't the first time Abby's been investigated in connection to a fire?"

Coldness hit William's core. He didn't, but he wasn't about to admit it. "Where did you learn that?"

"The reporter, Isabelle, called me. She had some questions."

And she called Joe, not William. William's hand shook as he rubbed his forehead. It suddenly became tremendously difficult to form a coherent thought. God had never fallen in line with William's expectations. His doubts about the divine had grown alongside his pain. The biblical truths he espoused in his youth failed to affect his heart after Claire's diagnosis. Grappling with her impending death shook him awake from spiritual apathy and into a search for God. He lost his wife. Ella lost her mom. William lost stability, and he'd been floundering for it ever since. It took a fair bit of counseling to learn how to live intentionally amidst the pain and to understand that God's greatest concern for William was to rescue him from his sin.

Taking hold of Gramps's care had temporarily returned purpose to his life. It had given William a new reason to get up in the morning. It gave him something to feel good about. But at what cost? Guilt heaped upon guilt. Abby had moved here for a job that would become nonexistent if Gramps returned to full-time care. Ella was finally thriving, and he'd have to rip her from another home if they lost the farm. Uncle Joe had been happy knowing Gramps was safe in the home, and William swooped in and pulled him out. But he had to believe that despite the attacks, fire, and threats, God had not relinquished control of the world once. To believe otherwise would be to deny Scripture. He inhaled a deep, pained breath.

Uncle Joe planted his elbows on the desk and steepled his fingers. He looked William dead in the eyes. "Clearly, Dad would be better off back in the home."

The last five seconds had been spent second guessing every decision he'd made. Still, William's instinctive response was no. "He wasn't happy there."

"Life isn't about happiness. Responsibility has to factor in somewhere." Joe's flattened lips etched doubt into every microexpression.

William folded his arms across his chest and tucked his hands into his armpits. "None of that changes the fact that you're dismissing him simply because he's old. You enjoy a quality of life. Why shouldn't Gramps?"

"Come on." Joe sucked in his cheeks. "Get your head out of the sand and open your eyes. The man lives and breathes conspiracy. Of course, I don't believe things were as bad as he said. But at least there, he'll be safe."

"He should be safe in this home."

"But he's not."

Joe was right. Gramps wasn't safe. None of them were. William blew out a noisy breath.

"What if Dad got lost in a memory and wandered to the cottage to sit in that rocker on the porch and enjoy a cigar like he used to? What if he dropped the cigar?" Joe lobbed the questions softly, but they landed with the momentum of a swinging baseball bat.

"Do you think Gramps started the fire?"

Color rose in Joe's cheeks. "Dad needs more care than you realize. This proves it."

William ground his molars together. If he relaxed his jaw, he wouldn't be able to control what might spew if his internal pressure valve blew. "Abby signed a contract. I can't put Gramps back in."

It was a weak argument. But after everything that had happened, he didn't know what else to say. *Lord, I don't know what to do. I want to be wise. But what's the wise choice?*

Uncle Joe pushed back from the desk and leaned back in the chair. "I say we let the girl go with a generous bonus for her trouble, resettle Gramps into the home, and then deal with the property."

The girl. Abby was more than just the hired girl.

"Where is she? We might as well get it over with."

William's head jerked. Uncle Joe wanted to do this now? He pressed a palm to his eyes and released a huge breath. "I gave her the day off. She and Carson went into town."

"Willy?"

The faint call drifted down the stairs. William fisted his hands. If he didn't go, Gramps would try to come to him. A stumble on the stairs in Joe's presence would only bolster Joe's arguments.

"I better see what he wants."

Uncle Joe stood with him and followed William to the door, reaching out to stop him. "I'm not the bad guy here. I care about him. He's my dad." Joe's voice cracked. "Michael and I weren't the best kids. We made a mess of things, and I know Dad doesn't trust me. Maybe he doesn't even like me. But I love him. The best place for him is a home where he gets round-the-clock care. I want him to be safe." Joe's voice cracked on the last word.

William's eyes watered. Not out of sympathy for Joe, although he sympathized. It was the mention of his father. Michael. The deadbeat dad who bailed after Mom got sick.

William's stomach pitched. Uncle Joe might not be the warmest man in the world, but at least he stayed. That counted for something. The pressure in William's head intensified and built up behind his eyes.

"Willy?"

"I gotta go." William took the stairs two at a time. He should have moved Gramps onto the main floor a long time ago. He'd have to get Abby to do that ASAP. "I'm coming, Gramps."

A creak on the old floorboards hitched his steps. He

stopped and listened. If Gramps was in the room to his right, there shouldn't be anyone down the hall.

He'd left Joe in the office. Rose and Ella were downstairs in the playroom. Abby and Carson were out. His muscles coiled. The tension in the air intensified. "Who's there?"

"Willy?" Gramps called again. "I need the restroom. I can't get out of bed."

William eyed the dark corridor. He saw nothing in the shadowy corners, but every hair on his body stood at attention. "Uncle Joe, can you come up here?"

"Willy?" Gramps sounded agitated.

"I'm coming."

Joe bounded up behind him. "What's up?"

As William turned to speak, a hooded figure burst from a spare bedroom. It shoved William into his uncle, pushed past them, and dashed down the stairs.

Joe stumbled. William tried to steady him, but he couldn't grab hold of him. Joe tumbled back. The thunderous banging of his body on the stairs echoed in the house.

"Uncle Joe!" William lurched toward the crumpled body at the bottom of the staircase.

"William?" Rose's faint call came from the direction of the playroom.

"I'm okay." Joe pushed himself into a sitting position. "I'll get Dad. Call the police. Check on Ella." Uncle Joe crawled toward the stairs and dragged himself up one slow step at a time.

William raced to the front of the house. "Rose? Ella?" *Please Lord, let them be safe.*

The front door hung ajar, and William nearly collapsed with relief. Whoever had been here was gone.

Rose rounded the corner, her hand clasping Ella's, who dragged a doll by one arm.

William sagged against the door frame.

Rose panted as if they'd run all the way.

"Take Ella to the playroom and lock the door from the inside. I have to call the police."

She nodded, her eyes so wide they nearly swallowed her head. She hurried Ella back the way they'd come, whispering to her the entire time.

William shut and locked the front door and raced back to Gramps's room. He shot through the bedroom door.

The bed was empty.

"Gramps?"

The toilet flushed. The faucet turned on. Gramps, supported by Uncle Joe, hobbled out of the ensuite bath. "I almost didn't make it."

CHAPTER

TEN

Carson's hand tucked into Abby's as they wandered Chenaniah River's main street. Several quaint businesses had propped their doors open so enticing displays could pull customers inside. Luscious hanging baskets suspended from old-fashioned street lamps, and town employees lifted hoses with long extensions to water the foliage. A tall clock stood erect in the center of the street. Abby had never heard the tower chime, but she imagined the sound to be glorious. Chenaniah River appeared to be everything the tourism brochures had promised. At least, it did on the surface.

"Ice cream?" Carson pointed to a diner with a strong 50s vibe, complete with steel counters, barstools, and a black-and-white checkered floor.

"A little later, okay? It's kind of early for ice cream."

They passed a few more storefronts—a high-end clothing store for women, an exclusive hat store, and a jeweler—before they reached the Niagara Gazette.

Abby's appointment with Isabelle was in five minutes. She'd hoped the reporter had better luck than she did. Abby wasn't any closer to uncovering what was going on than she'd been before the fire. She'd hoped Austin would have been able to provide some insight, but a quick phone call to him earlier that morning had revealed his illness was worsening. She brought him up to date about the drugs and the fire, and suggested he get a toxicology screen specific to what that chemist cooked. She'd worked with influenza patients long enough to recognize his symptoms were more than a stomach bug or food poisoning, and if their old friend had found Abby, he could also find Austin. When she finished with Austin, she called Dr. Pike and asked him to order labs for Gramps. Maybe his continued stomach pain was more than a sensitive digestive system?

Abby pushed through the double front doors of the office space tucked in between a bank ATM and a variety store.

A perky receptionist looked up when the bell over the door jingled. She had a phone clamped between her ear and shoulder. "Can I help you?"

"I have an appointment with one of your reporters. Isabelle Barlow." Abby could see the work area behind reception. Four desks were pushed together. A jacket hung off the back of a chair, and sticky notes plastered one computer monitor.

The receptionist jotted down a note and ended her call. "Isabelle was called out, but she said to give you this." The receptionist handed Abby a folded note. A grainy broadcast from the police scanner on the receptionist's desk blared. Her cheeks reddened as she turned the volume down.

So that's how they knew to send Isabelle to the fire. Someone must monitor the police scanner 24/7.

According to the note, Isabelle's boss sent her to the fairgrounds. "Which way is Memorial Park? Isabelle asked me to meet her at the fair."

The receptionist pointed left. "Take a left out the doors, and a right on Broad Street."

"That's super helpful. Thank you." Abby squeezed Carson's hand as they stepped back into the sunshine. "Looks like we are checking out the fair. What do you think about that?"

"We play games?" Carson lifted his eyebrows with a hopeful expression.

"I'm not sure, Sweetheart. It might not be open yet. I think Rose said something about the fair opening later this week. They could still be setting up."

Carson's lip protruded.

"But watching the big machines that build the rides will be fun."

Carson added a bit of skip to his step.

It didn't take long to find Isabelle. She was snapping photographs and chatting up workers. Her hair was pulled back into a ponytail. She wore little makeup, not that her creamy skin needed it. Some women would want to cover the freckles that smattered across her cheeks, but Isabelle didn't seem to mind them. Abby liked her right away. She waved her free hand.

Isabelle excused herself from a conversation with the man unloading mirrors from a truck. A second man stacked the mirrors; they were the warped kind you might find in a funhouse. A third guy hauled them into a makeshift building.

Isabelle smiled as she approached. "Thanks for coming to me. Sorry about the last-minute change."

Abby motioned to a nearby bench. Just coming here so

Isabelle could give her the scoop felt like a betrayal of the family she'd come to love, but her loyalty had to lie with Carson and no one else. "Did you learn anything more?"

As they sat down, Carson wandered a few feet away and stretched onto his belly. He poked at an insect in the grass.

Isabelle lowered her voice so Carson couldn't hear. "It's been an enlightening week." But instead of dishing, Isabelle cocked her head to the side like a curious bird and volleyed the question back. "What did you find?"

"I dug into the staff. Jethro has been with the orchard for nearly two decades. I don't know if it's in writing, but Gramps had promised that if the orchard ever sold, Jethro would be taken care of. It's possible that Jethro could want that inheritance now. Especially if he's concerned Gramps is losing his mind. Rose's sister is ill. She needs this job, so I don't see an upside to her manipulating things, unless William made her a similar promise. I also left a message for William's dad." A rather long message she regretted the second she'd left it. But it was done now.

"I also did a bit of digging."

Abby leaned in.

"This isn't the first fire you've experienced."

Tension swirled in Abby's chest. Isabelle looked into her? Of course, she learned about the fire that killed her parents. She probably also knew about the insurance payout Abby was set to receive on her thirtieth birthday. Her parents' will had stipulated the funds be kept in a trust for her until then.

But this wasn't about her. "Yes. I lost my parents. And I'll do anything to ensure that Carson never has to experience something like that."

Isabelle must have seen something she liked because her

chin lifted and moved on. "I also discovered that Joe frequents local casinos."

"Joe's a gambler?"

"According to my research, not a very good one."

Abby leaned back on the park bench. Every family had a few skeletons in its closet, but this was more than a secret or two. First, speculation about Gramps laundering money for organized crime at worst or evading taxes at best. Then, hidden alcoholism with William's dad. And now Joe's a gambler? Their skeletons were multiplying into a boneyard. "And what about William? Does he have any connections to organized crime?"

Someone turned on the funhouse music, and Abby winced. The carnival soundtrack dialed back to a more tolerable decibel, but Isabelle still had to yell to be heard. "He doesn't have enough money to be connected to them. I have no proof, so this is totally off the record, but the orchard is nearly broke."

"Broke?" Abby covered her ears with her hands. The only thing she hated more than carnival music was clowns.

"I ran with that one, trying to find out if there was an insurance policy attached to the cottage that would pay out."

"And?" Abby held her breath.

"It's enough to be a motive."

Abby's stomach flipped. William was broke? Even if a payout went directly into William's pocket, she'd never believe he'd do something so terrible. He wouldn't burn down the cottage to save the orchard. Not while she and Carson were in it.

"I appreciate you speaking with me so candidly." The carousel behind them started to turn, and its music competed with the funhouse. The early pangs of a headache pierced her skull. "Carson and I will let you get back to work." She glanced at where Carson had been playing. He was gone.

"Carson?" She leaped to her feet. He was right there. "Did you see where he went?"

"No." Isabelle spun in a slow circle.

All around them, crews of people hauled crates and boxes. Machinery beeped. Hammers pounded. Carousels spun. Funhouses beckoned.

Abby cupped her hands around her lips. "Carson!"

A faint cry sounded from inside the slapped-together building where the men had been hauling the mirrors. Abby rushed into the maze while Isabelle explained the situation to the man out front. A hundred Abbys reflected in the mirrors. Then, a hundred Isabelles, and hundreds more of men she'd never met. They'd never find Carson like this. "Carson!"

Each turn drew her deeper into the maze. Someone cut the funhouse music, and an eerie silence dropped. The sounds of scuffling feet just behind the walls of mirrors dulled the chance of hearing her baby's voice. She turned another corner. *Carson!*

He swiped a hand over his runny nose. A giant tear slid down his cheek. She rushed forward and slammed into a mirror. It was a reflection. She spun around. A hand yanked Carson to the side, and he disappeared.

"Carson!" she screamed.

"I have him," a voice called out. A calm voice. A kind voice. "I'm bringing him out the back." The footsteps faded.

Abby spun again. She had to find the exit. But every path she took led to a dead end. Her heart galloped. Her breaths shortened. She couldn't seem to get enough oxygen to her brain to think clearly. Why couldn't she find the exit? Where did everyone else go? All she saw in the mirrors was her own reflection.

Another turn, another mirror. "I need help," she called.

Footsteps shuffled on the other side.

"I feel so silly. This is a child's game, but I can't seem to find—"

A shadow rose behind her. The reflection made it hard to tell which direction it came from. The large form stepped closer, and then she saw it. A clown with a painted-on red smile that hid a sinister sneer.

"You should have gone home. Now you'll pay."

Incomprehension blurred the edges of her vision. She stumbled against the mirror.

The clown stepped closer. He raised his hands. Her mind denied what was unfolding. This wasn't real. Her ears roared. She blinked, trying to clear the fuzz in her head. The cheap mirror felt cool against her back. Everything shifted to black and white. Like an old movie.

Shock transformed into panic.

The clown took another step. It wasn't face paint. It was a mask. A clown mask that exposed only the eyes.

Dark, piercing, angry eyes.

A growl erupted from deep within her. She swung and stumbled.

The clown snickered.

A sharp pain split her cheek. The acrid tang of blood. Fingers wrapped around her neck and squeezed, crushing her windpipe. Piercing pain cut through her skull.

Abby grasped at the clown's fingers and pulled back two of them. Black spots danced, but she heard a bone crack and a howl.

The grip on her neck loosened, and she thrust her shoulder to the side and broke his hold. She stumbled back. Before she could shift from defensive to offensive, the clown turned and ran.

ANXIETY CLAWED at the back of William's throat. He snapped Ella's car seat buckles together and tightened them.

"Ouchie!" Ella arched her back and pushed against the straps.

His hands stilled. William forced his mind to slow, and he took a mindful breath. Isabelle contacted him because Abby had no one else to call. Carson was inconsolable and needed a familiar face. The three milliseconds he'd gain by rushing would not have an impact that made it worth it.

He loosened the buckle and leaned into the backseat, pressing his lips to Ella's forehead. "All better?"

She grinned that goofy grin he loved more than life.

It took an astronomical effort to force himself to drive the speed limit to pick up Abby and Carson. He lectured himself. Thirty seconds wouldn't change anything. Getting into an accident on the way won't help. He had to trust the Lord held them in His palm.

"We go to the fair!" Ella clapped her hands from her car seat in the back as the peak of the Ferris wheel came into view.

"It's not open yet. We are just picking up Carson and Abby." He would have preferred to leave Ella at the house, but after the break-in, Rose got a call from her sister, and he told her to go to her. The poor woman was a wreck. He half expected her resignation in the morning. William brought Ella along with him and left Gramps with Uncle Joe, who, although banged up from his fall, seemed okay. The police were on their way. Again.

He squeezed his eyes shut for a millisecond. Lord, give me strength.

After paying for a prime parking spot near two police cars, he helped Ella out of her car seat. The town had grown around the park. Every mayor had protected the green space in the middle of the village. It boasted a fountain in which children splashed on hot days, several park benches, paths that led to the lake in one direction and to the cultural center in the other direction. Once a year, a small fair set up, attracting locals to the tourist strip.

It wasn't hard to find Abby and Carson. Officers Andy Reuben and Gavin Thorn sat with Abby, one on either side of her. Carson stood in front of his mom, eyes glued to her face.

William's heart hiccuped as tears dripped from Carson's chin.

Andy took notes as Abby spoke. She pressed an ice pack to the back of her head with one hand and gestured with the other hand.

"Carson!" Ella pulled her hand free and waved wildly. She skipped toward her friend, oblivious to the tension in the air.

Carson turned their way. His countenance lit up when he saw Ella. And when Carson's eyes bounced off Ella's and found his, William's entire body relaxed. The relief on Carson's face shifted something inside of him. It made William feel like a man, a protector, and a father.

Abby's posture communicated a very different reaction. Their eyes met, then her gaze darted sideways and down. But not before he glimpsed her shame and fear.

William dropped to a knee in front of Abby. He rubbed

circles on Carson's back, but he focused on her. "Are you okay?"

She nodded. Her eyes pinched as if she were in pain. The beginnings of a bruise started on her throat, but she was here. He hadn't lost her. The tension bottled inside of him evaporated as he drank her in like a thirsty man.

Ella tugged on Carson's hand and pointed at the play equipment a few feet away. Before she could ask, Officer Gavin stood. "I'll watch them."

"Thanks," William said. "Mommy's safe," he said to Carson, as if he knew what fears swirled in the boy's heart.

It's like they were a family. Carson carried the weight of being the man of the house until William arrived to take over. Even Abby, as capable and strong as she was, leaned into his strength as if it were a life preserver. How had she drilled so deeply into their hearts? She'd become such an important part of Ella and Gramps's life.

He pretended it was all about Ella and Gramps, but he felt the twang deep in his chest. He was falling in love with a woman who had snuck into town to question a reporter about his family.

She probably had no idea that Isabelle spoke with Uncle Joe about her.

"I'm okay. I just feel stupid." She refused to meet his gaze.

"Isabelle told me what you asked her. You could have come to me. I would have answered your questions."

Abby winced. She moved tenderly, as if she had a pounding headache. But as serious as her physical injuries were, William was more concerned about her emotional ones. Why hadn't she been able to come to him? Why did she feel the need to sneak around to find answers?

Isabelle jogged up from the parking lot. "I had a bottle in

my car." She shook two pills into her palm, which he assumed were over-the-counter pain medication, and she handed them to Abby.

Abby popped them into her mouth and swallowed without needing liquid to get them down. "You shouldn't have come," she said to William. "I could have driven home."

His chuckle did not amuse her, but she had to hear the ridiculousness of her statement. It reminded him of the time he had his wisdom teeth out. The painkillers didn't make him weepy or loopy like they did with others. They made him overconfident. He spent the entire ride home telling Gramps he could have driven himself because putting gasoline in an engine was a mechanical miracle and the car would drive itself.

"You're not driving home." Isabelle folded her arms across her chest. "You have Carson to think about. That's why I called William."

All Abby ever did was think about Carson. The blow to her head must have been harder than William realized if Isabelle had to step in to help Abby regain her focus.

"I'm fine. The EMT said I'm fine. The police took the report. We're fine." Abby's attention shifted to Carson, where he squatted beside Ella and they poked at something in the dirt.

Three *fines* strung together like that meant a person was not fine, despite trying to prove they were.

"There is a difference between fine as in not dead and fine as in capable of operating heavy machinery. Carson wandering off into the funhouse and needing the amusement park staff to find him is scary enough," Isabelle said. "But that's just a kid being a kid. Someone attacking you…

that means someone followed you, watched you, and wants to hurt you."

Abby paled further at Isabelle's words, and William's lungs cemented.

"I don't know what's going on, but I know when something is not *fine*." Isabelle put air quotes around the word fine.

Abby stood just as a pop sliced the air. Isabelle's body jerked and crumpled.

William's first thought was firecrackers, followed immediately by the ridiculousness of that idea.

"Gun!" Abby screamed.

Another crack slammed into the wooden slats by Isabelle. Splinters shot out like a sunburst from a hole.

Abby hooked her hands under Isabelle's arms and dragged her to cover.

William spun and dove in one fluid motion. Adrenaline coursed through him. In the space of a single breath, the fairgrounds transformed into chaos. Everything went too slowly and too fast at the same time. He just needed to reach the kids. He had to get to the kids.

Bodies and bullets. Flaring nostrils and screams. But all he saw was the ground around the children that popped with mini eruptions. William tackled them like a linebacker. His outstretched arms curled the children into his body. He covered them and braced for the inevitable hit. *Lord, protect them!*

Gavin positioned himself on one knee in front of them, gun raised, shielding their cowering bodies, looking for the shooter.

The thudding of bullets embedding in the nearby tree

trunks rattled in William's ears. He tightened his hold on their whimpering frames. *Take me, Lord. Not the kids.*

Abby yanked his arm. "Over here!" She was trying to pull him and the kids toward the spot she'd left Isabelle. Trying to jolt him from his frozen stupor.

Gavin shouted, "Go!" He covered them as a sudden silence descended that was just as horrifying as the unexpected panic from seconds before.

Another pop. The dirt around his feet dusted.

Pop. A carnival worker dropped a few feet from them. He writhed on the ground, grasping his arm. Red seeped.

Ella screamed. She buried her face in his chest.

"Don't look, baby. Keep your eyes closed."

Abby pulled on William until his legs worked. He crawled with the kids until he was behind a large piece of equipment. He sank to the ground, running his hands up and down Ella first and then Carson. They were unhurt.

He couldn't say the same for Isabelle. He couldn't look away from her gray face and bloodstained shirt. The tiniest rise and fall assured him she was still alive.

Carson's hands pressed against his ears, and he squeezed his eyes shut. Tears streamed from the corners. Ella's raspy breaths and bulging eyes increased as she clawed at him for a better hold. William squeezed her.

"The shot came from that direction." Abby pointed to the second story of a haunted house. "Stay here."

Carson lunged for his mother, and William pulled him back.

Abby re-entered the fray.

William pulled Carson's face into his shoulder and rotated so he couldn't see. Ella curled into him. His mind fought to keep up with his galloping heartbeat.

Lord!

It was all he could manage. Confusion abounded as innocents sought cover. Except for Abby.

Lord, please.

She ran toward the chaos. She grabbed the fabric of the downed man's shirt and started dragging him their way.

"Stay here," William instructed the kids.

"No, Daddy!" Ella's scream cut to his heart.

He peeled desperate little hands from him and made the stupidest decision of his life. *Lord, please.*

He grabbed a fistful of material and helped Abby pull the man to safety.

A ping hit the machinery providing them cover. William winced and hunkered down even more. Ella threw herself at him, sobbing. Carson sat stone-still, frozen. In shock.

Abby assessed the fallen man's wound. "You'll be fine." She bent forward so she could look into the panicked man's eyes. "It just grazed you. Probably burns like crazy, but you'll be okay. Keep pressure on it."

Officer Andy Reuben was preparing to enter the building Abby had pointed at earlier. Abby's body readied, and he understood her intention. William latched onto her upper arm and matched the pressure compressing his heart. "Don't."

CHAPTER
ELEVEN

Abby jerked her arm, but she couldn't shake William free. His fingers dug into her soft flesh.

"Don't," he repeated.

One word. Within that single syllable lay meaning. Why did it take something like this for her to see his heart? She should have gone to him and asked her questions about his dad. She shouldn't have roped in Isabelle. Maybe then, Isabelle wouldn't have been shot.

Her gaze dropped to the kids clinging to him, one glued to each leg, crying. He was such a good man. William's free hand rested on Carson's head and stroked his hair. Her little boy's body shuddered with each breath. His over-bright eyes begged her to stay. Carson needed a man like William in his life.

What was she doing? She wasn't a police officer anymore. She had no obligation to serve and protect anyone but the children in front of her. Why did she feel this desperate need to face her attacker head-on? Why couldn't she allow others to fight this battle? Why couldn't she trust God and keep Him first? Why wasn't she satisfied just being Carson's mom? Ella's role model? William's—

She didn't know what she was to William. But with sudden clarity, she knew she wanted to be more.

Her heart seized. Her mind replayed the last few seconds. A soft roar buzzed in her ears. William had grabbed Carson. When she couldn't get to him, he protected Carson and shielded him with his body.

The roar swelled from gentle waves to a raging surf. The man she questioned Isabelle about, the one she doubted, the one whose character she called into question. How could she have ever been unsure that William Roth was a good man?

"Let the police handle it," he pressed. "You're not a cop anymore. You're a mother. A—" He stopped.

Her insides froze. Everything blurred. What was he going to say? Who was she to him, and why did it matter that they define it?

"A friend." His eyes dampened. "You're a friend."

Disappointment coursed through her. She wanted to be so much more.

Carson hiccuped. His teeth bit down on his bottom lip. His little chin pressed into his chest as he burrowed into William's leg.

This was why she left the force. She couldn't take the chance she'd leave Carson alone. But a fresh possibility that she'd never considered rolled over her. What if she was left behind?

A repeat of history rose as a distinct possibility. God might allow the enemy to steal from her the one person she loved more than anything—Carson. Abby curled her arms above her head and moaned. How could she stay here and watch while a gunman picked off people? She couldn't stand on the sidelines when she could be part of the solution. Especially in a small town with limited resources.

"You don't have a weapon," William built his argument as if the conflicting emotions scrolled across her face like a teleprompter. "There is nothing you can do to help them. But staying means everything to us."

He was so close, but he sounded far away. It was like she'd detached from her body and observed the scene as if it were a movie.

Isabelle moaned.

"She needs you," William said, nodding toward Isabelle. "I don't know how to help them."

Most people had vacated the scene or found hiding spots, hunched behind vehicles. Some had run into the nearby houses as neighbors opened their homes so people could shelter in place. But Isabelle and the unfortunate worker weren't so lucky.

Useless observations piled one on top of the other. Ella rocking in place. The trembling in William's hand. His shaky voice. The manic energy coursing through her body. It made little sense. How could she think about these things while a gunman terrorized them?

Fear gripped her and squeezed until there was nothing left. "Keep pressure on his wound," she told William, nodding at the carnival worker. She turned to Isabelle. It was a through and through. Upper shoulder.

Abby's hand trembled as she pressed against the wound. Isabelle groaned.

"I know it hurts. We have to slow the bleeding."

Isabelle's eyes pinched.

William murmured to the injured man. The kids still

clung to him. And it hit her. She didn't have to do this alone. An uncontrollable sob built in her chest. That's when the shaking started. They could have been killed. All of them.

Or even worse, all of them except her. She wouldn't survive another loss like that.

She didn't know how long they were like that. Others joined their hiding spot. The police returned empty-handed. The shooter had escaped. At least the injuries were minor. Either the shooter was an awful shot, or he missed on purpose.

It was all a game to him, a game she didn't want to play anymore.

The paramedics arrived. They rushed Isabelle and the injured man to Grand River Hospital. As they pulled away, Abby sagged into William, and he wrapped his arms around her. He rocked back and forth, holding the three of them. Her and their kids. He pressed his lips to her hair and whispered over and over that it was going to be okay. He didn't have the power to make it true, but he said it anyway, and she wanted to believe him. Lightheadedness made her head swim. A chill washed over her, and her shaking turned to tremors. She couldn't gain control of her body. Her ears rang. Her vision tunneled. She felt numb.

It wouldn't be okay. It might never be okay again. Turning the drugs over to the police didn't stop the rampage. Somebody had followed her and targeted her in the funhouse. And they did it while she had Carson. Isabelle was the first person shot. Likely the intended target. Was that because she spoke with Abby? Was everyone connected to Abby in danger?

Carson climbed into her lap. Ella curled into her shoulder. William pulled her back against his chest, and she felt safe. Dampness chilled her cheeks. She stroked Ella's hair. They were lucky. This could have ended differently.

No, not lucky. Luck implied that God was not in control. But as awful and random as it felt, God had control the entire time. He was able—with a single word—to stop it all. But He didn't.

She'd been afraid her entire adult life that God would take more from her than she could stand. Ever since her parents died, she'd wrestled, knowing that God had given the nod for her life to unfold the way it had. What if He took Carson or William? He might take everything that mattered to her because the Creator had the freedom to do whatever He pleased with His creation.

But balancing the other side of that scale was an understanding that her call to suffer had come from a God who loved her with a tenderness that was perfect and holy and without sin. She didn't understand how the two sides meshed together, but she trusted what she knew of the character of God. He loved her. He'd always loved her.

The pressure of William's hands anchored her. William crushed her against him, and the kids wiggled in between. His soft prayers whispered into her hair. He stood to lose the same things that she did. William had no guarantee that today would end well for him. He didn't know if he'd bring his little girl home tonight. But instead of questioning God, instead of wailing about how huge the trial was and how unfair the struggle felt, he told the enemy how big his God was.

William prayed, "God, you are good. Even here. Even now. I trust you, and no matter what the day brings, I will praise you. Give us strength to endure and faith to believe. Give us courage. Keep us safe."

Any lingering doubts about William vanished. He whispered this prayer over them, a prayer so intimate, powerful, and meaningful that she knew they were beginning something together that held the potential to change both their lives. She let his strength seep into her bones. She wasn't alone. She had William.

If they survived the day.

Her muscles quivered and anger roused so intense that it frightened her. Who had targeted her? Who had it in for Gramps? It had to stop before more people got hurt. She just didn't know how to stop it.

"Lord, one day You will right this wrong and dry every tear. Joy will replace our sorrow. Certainty will replace our fear. Justice will prevail. Until that day, use this crushing pain to remind us that nothing on earth will satisfy us. Only heaven can."

Her lungs filled. She held it as long as she could, and a peace that she couldn't describe replaced her anxiety. Her breath whistled out. Her racing heart slowed. They stayed there, huddled together, for over an hour. Her damp forehead tingled. William never let up the pressure while he held her. Her throbbing heartbeat in her eardrums lessened. A final, deep breath put her back in the driver's seat of her emotions. They made it. They survived.

William tracked her every movement. She nodded an answer to his unasked question. She was going to be okay. The muscles in his expression loosened a bit until she asked, "Why?"

William knew she wasn't asking him. She was asking God. She was asking God the one question she had refused to ask Him her entire life. Why?

The warmth of William's hands remained. He never pulled away. Her question didn't scare him.

"God hates evil because He hates sin. Today is the work of the enemy, but God will steer it for His purposes."

She didn't respond. She knew William was preaching to his own heart as much as he was speaking to hers. Like Job from the Bible, Abby had to decide if the God who gives and takes away was worthy of her love.

HOURS HAD PASSED. William had called Uncle Joe to check in on Gramps, and he was doing fine. The police had yet to arrive regarding the break-in. Every officer in town and more from the nearby larger cities swarmed the area where the shooting took place. Officers conducted interviews, searched buildings, collected evidence, and offered first aid. They would interview Gramps and Uncle Joe later. A break-in with no major injuries wasn't high enough on the priority list today.

Every fiber of Abby's being had to be pulsating with a desire to be part of the response that buzzed around them, but she stayed by his side the entire time.

For Carson and Ella.

For him?

William carried Ella on his hip as they spoke with the police officers. Abby held Carson. Despite Abby's policing background, they wouldn't share the details of their investigation beyond confirming there was a man in custody. After what felt like forever, the police finally gave them permission to leave.

William offered his arm to Abby.

She looped her hand over the crook of his elbow. She wilted a little, swaying a bit with each step.

He got it. Exhaustion crashed down on him too, weighing down his limbs and making his eyes scratchy. "I'll bring you home. We can come back for your car later."

Home. Did she think of the orchard as home? She had nothing holding her here. He couldn't blame her if she left. There was only so much a person could take before cracking. Abby had to be pressing her limits.

Her phone beeped. Abby's lips twisted into a weak smile. "Isabelle is in surgery. They expect her to be okay."

William's steps hitched. Right. Isabelle. Abby had met with the reporter to discuss William and his family. After everything that had happened, he'd forgotten the reason she was at the park. Abby didn't trust him.

William rolled his neck and shoulders, but it failed to loosen the tension. They got the kids into the car, having moved Carson's car seat into the back of William's vehicle. The normalcy of their motions screamed. How could they carry on as if this day were only a blip on the radar? They looked like a normal family, but they were anything but normal. William assisted Abby into the front. At best, they were a family in need of intense counseling. At worst, they were moving targets for the psycho tormenting them.

William almost laughed at the kids chattering in the backseat. Children recovered so much quicker than adults. He was torn between wanting to scream that they should be scared, terrified like he was, but he was also thankful they bounced back. The two extremes battled for control as he put the vehicle in gear and headed home.

"Thank you for coming," Abby whispered.

"Did you really think I wouldn't?" He didn't need her to

answer the question. The fact she thanked him provided the information. She hadn't expected him to come when Isabelle called. It crushed him she thought so little of him after all they'd endured together.

A faint pink colored Abby's neck. She turned to look out the window. He should leave it alone, but he couldn't.

"Why didn't you come to me? Why involve Isabelle?" William's grip tightened on the steering wheel. He straightened his fingers and then flexed them, trying to loosen the knots in his hands. But nothing would loosen the knot in his stomach. He was so thankful Abby and Carson were okay. He was grateful to be driving her home. Relieved that she stayed with him and the kids and didn't run into the building with the police officers. But now that the danger was over, now that they were safe, frustration reared its ugly head. She had no right to poke into his history and dig up dirt from his past. What was she thinking, stoking the curiosity of a reporter?

"You're angry." She said it without turning her head. She still looked out the window. But the vulnerability in her posture and tone softened his core.

He held his breath for a moment before answering. "Honestly, yes. You crossed a line." She didn't just cross it. She jumped so far past it that the line was a dot in her rear-view mirror.

Abby turned toward him as if she were going to meet his gaze, but at the last minute, she dropped her eyes and focused on her hands. They fidgeted in her lap, pulling at a loose thread on the cuff of her shirt. She didn't apologize.

He blew out a noisy breath. "You should have asked me. Then, you wouldn't have been there when the shooting started. You would have been home with me. Safe."

"Home hasn't proven to be any safer."

He groaned, but couldn't deny the truth in her words. More than anything else, he wanted to protect her, but he didn't know how. "While you were out, someone broke into the house. They were in the hallway outside Gramps's room."

A sharp intake of breath was her only sound. Her posture stiffened as she worked through the meaning. There was more going on than they had considered. This was bigger than her.

"We can't be dealing with just one guy. He couldn't have been downtown shooting up the fairgrounds and at the farm breaking into the house. We have two separate problems." As if one wasn't enough.

"If they can still get that close to Gramps, we're not safe anywhere." She rubbed her hands up and down her arms as a shiver rippled down her frame.

He wasn't trying to scare her, but maybe she needed to be scared. Maybe she and Carson needed to leave Chenaniah River? He didn't want to lose her, but he'd rather she left and be safe than stay and be in danger. Maybe he should suggest she take Ella and Gramps and hide away until they figure out what is going on. But what if the trouble followed her? If it did, she'd have to face it alone.

It was as if she could read his mind. "We have to figure out what's going on. It's the only way we'll be safe."

He flicked his gaze to the backseat via the rear-view mirror. Thankfully, the kids were not tracking their conversation. They'd nodded off. Their heads bobbed with each dip and sway of the vehicle.

He rubbed a hand along his jaw and then slid it around to the back of his neck. Abby was right. It wasn't any safer in the house. "And how do we do that?"

"It's part of the reason I spoke with Isabelle. I'm trying to figure out how the pieces fit together."

"Why did you go to her instead of asking me what you wanted to know?"

Her complexion reddened. She shifted her gaze away. "I realized I don't know that much about you and your family. I packed up and moved across the province on a job offer and a basic internet search. I should have done better. I should have looked closer at who I was allowing into Carson's life."

Her answer slammed into him with unexpected force. Who she allowed into Carson's life? It's like she thought they were some crime family. "I know we're not perfect, but—"

"Did you know that Uncle Joe has a gambling problem?" she interjected.

He jerked his head back and turned away so she couldn't see his face. He didn't know, but he wasn't about to tell her that. "I don't see how that's any of your business."

"And Gramps fudged the books back when he was running things?"

"No way," he blurted. "I took over the business, and I would have noticed." His gut rolled over. A sudden and unwelcome thought followed that one. If she discovered that about Uncle Joe and Gramps, what did she learn about him? Was it enough to make her want to leave? Did it make her suspect he was just as morally corrupt as she thought the others were? Did she also uncover the orchard's growing debt? What else crawled out from under the rocks she lifted? They weren't a perfect family. He knew that better than anyone, but they deserved better than this.

His muscles tightened. There was a jerkiness in his movements that he couldn't control. He parked in front of the house. Uncle Joe's truck was gone, and he stifled a frustrated sigh. The least he could have done was wait until William had returned before leaving Gramps alone. Especially after all that had happened. But maybe it was for the best. If Joe were here, Abby might want to speak with him about the gambling debt, and William didn't have the bandwidth to do that right now.

Abby got out of the car and opened the back door to help Carson. She shook him awake. "It's time to get out."

Ella stirred at the noise, but William remained frozen in the front seat. After everything they'd been through, Abby believed the worst about his family. All without giving him a chance to enter the conversation.

"Are you coming?" Abby had Carson perched on her hip.

She embodied everything he thought he wanted in a woman. She was strong. Capable. Smart. But those were the very qualities that put a shovel in her hand and forced her to dig into his family. He thrust his fingers into his hair. "I need a bit of time. I'm going to go for a drive."

"I want to play with Carson." Now fully awake, Ella whined and pulled at her seat belt.

William tipped his head back against the seat. The tightness in his body wouldn't release. "Ella—"

"I can watch her," Abby said softly. "She's no trouble."

Ella sucked in her belly and leaned forward, as far as the seat belt would let her. She clasped her hands under her chin, holding still in expectation. He'd be able to work through his emotions with the Lord much easier if he were alone.

"Fine."

Ella and Carson cheered as Abby walked around to the other side of the vehicle to help Ella out of the car. The minute she put Ella's feet on the ground, the kids scampered indoors.

Abby waited by his window.

He lowered the glass, but didn't speak. There wasn't anything left to say. He didn't know how he felt. He just knew he needed some space to gather his thoughts, or he risked saying something he'd regret.

"I'm sorry," she said. "I understand my questions feel like an intrusion. But if our roles were reversed, wouldn't you have done the same to be sure Ella was safe?"

He would have. But it didn't make him feel any better. "I just need some time."

She bounced her palm off the frame of the door and stepped back with a nod. She understood and didn't judge him for it. She waited in the driveway as he pulled away, watching him go. A part of him couldn't help but feel like he was leaving his future behind, like he was giving up on something special. But he didn't know what else to do.

CHAPTER
TWELVE

A hollowness carved out Abby's insides as William drove away. The grim twist of his mouth as he said goodbye gutted her. She wanted to defend herself for asking Isabelle to dig into his family, but at her core, she knew she'd betrayed him. Even before the shooting, his smile never reached his eyes.

But speaking with Isabelle was necessary. Picking history's scabs always hurts. Sure, she'd learned some valuable information, but at what cost? She shook her head. For the first time, she questioned her methods. She wasn't a cop investigating. She was a friend. And friends were direct, not sneaky. Until now, she'd had no one else to consider when making these sorts of decisions. Every choice was about her or what was best for Carson. Now, there was another adult involved that mattered, another adult who had ideas and dreams and feelings. She hated that she'd let William down.

Abby waited until William's vehicle turned onto the road and disappeared. She moved toward the house. It loomed large and represented everything she wanted for Carson. Even the open front door and the absentmindedness of it remaining ajar made her smile. Kids, plural, too busy thinking about playing to remember to close the door. She'd always wanted more than one child, and Ella was such a sweet girl. Her chest pinched. Was it possible that she could have found her happy ending here with the Roth family if she hadn't gone poking around where she didn't belong?

Her eyes drifted closed for a moment. What would it be like to come home to this place and a man like William and be part of a family like his? What would change if she weren't just employed here but belonged? Sure, she'd uncovered some warts, but nothing that made her suspect William was less than he presented himself to be. People came with history. Her history might even read worse. Lost her parents as a teen and potentially at fault. Pregnant out of wedlock. Barely into her new career as a police officer before quitting. Moving across the country to work with a man she failed to scrutinize.

She practically flaked off the paper. If she wanted William to believe the best about her, she had to extend the same grace to him. His family's mistakes were not his mistakes. When he returned, she'd apologize. She'd touch his hand, meet his eyes, and lean into everything he'd been offering, but she'd been afraid to accept.

Her belly flip-flopped. She was done playing house. It was time to deal with their feelings for each other.

She closed the front door behind her and stepped into the foyer. "Gramps? Carson?"

The television blared from the next room. There should be other noises. She clutched her arms to her chest. There should be chatter, laughter, and squeals from wherever the kids played. Her elbows pressed into her sides. Shakiness started in her lower limbs and moved upward.

This was ridiculous. She was overreacting because of the shooting. Still, her heartbeat quickened. It thudded in her chest, slamming against her rib cage with increasing momentum. A hum grew in her ears. Everything was fine. She'd step into the room and see that everything was fine. She moved along the wall, padding along, but they wouldn't have heard her even if she stomped. The television was too loud. That was why they didn't hear her.

But Gramps never listened to it that loud.

She quickened her pace. What if something was wrong? What if it was the same kind of wrong that had been tormenting them for days? She slipped her phone out of her pocket and dialed William, but disconnected before the call could engage. What would she say? He couldn't have the space he needed because his grandfather turned up the volume on the television?

Her eyes darted to the corners, looking for clues, assurances, safety. She'd convinced herself by the time she rounded the corner that she'd find Gramps struggling to remember which button was for the volume on the remote. The excitement from earlier was making her paranoid. Everything was fine. They were safe.

She forced herself to exhale.

But if that were true, why didn't the lump in her midsection dissolve? Why did sourness sting the back of her throat where bile simmered? Why did every instinct she'd cultivated as a police officer scream at her? With everything that had happened, she had to consider the possibility that they had some unfriendly company. She had to be ready. She slipped into William's office and took a letter opener off the desk. Stuffing it up her sleeve and fisting her hands at her side, she sucked in a breath. She strode toward the family room. "What are you watch—"

A man sat on a footstool, one child on each knee and a gun trained on Gramps. Gramps's face was ashen; the kids, frozen. "Do you remember me?"

Her mouth dried. "I saw you at the rest stop. You gave Carson his bear."

"And you didn't recognize me. That was your second mistake."

"Second?"

"Your first was standing by while children's services took my kids."

The memory erupted like a volcano. Devin Teale, the man she arrested for cooking drugs and pressing pills. The man swore revenge when children's services took his kids. She couldn't get enough air into her lungs. Why didn't she ask William to come inside? Why didn't she insist that the police check on Gramps? Why didn't she let the call go through? *Stupid, stupid, stupid.* She reached for the spot on her hip where she used to carry her service weapon. Her stomach lurched.

"Sit down, Officer Abigail Sinclair. It's time you and I had a little talk." Devin motioned to the armchair with the muzzle of the weapon.

"Why did you put the drugs into the bear?" Abby needed to establish her control over their interaction.

"That cop was watching me. I needed a backup plan to move the merchandise and your boy provided the perfect cover." He pointed the gun at Carson.

Abby's fingers twitched as her leg muscles tightened. She'd brought a letter opener to a gun fight. The pistol he waved was one of the most popular handguns in the country. It was available in several calibers and sizes. The slim, single-stack weapon was designed for concealed carry. It all came rushing back, her training, her knowledge, her fears.

"You made it harder than I expected to get them back," Devin chuckled. "By the time I had the pills, I was having so much fun with you that I wasn't ready to move on."

"Was it you at the park?" It came out scratchy, and she flinched at her exposed vulnerability.

"Let's not waste time on chitchat. We have a lot to cover." Devin's steady, lower pitch indicated he felt in control. That was good. It made him more stable. More confident. That could help her.

Her bones refused to release their tension. He wasn't wearing a mask. That wasn't a good sign. It meant that it didn't matter if they saw him, which meant that he didn't intend to leave any witnesses.

Fear singed her throat. She swallowed, but it didn't move. A fluttery feeling spun through her body. She licked her upper lip, unsure she had enough moisture in her mouth to speak. "Let the children go. This is between you and me."

He waved his gun again, and his face reddened. "You're the one who involved the children back when you helped the government take mine away."

Dread crawled over her skin. This was about revenge. He wanted nothing from her except to cause her pain. The same pain she caused him.

The revelation nearly buckled her knees. She couldn't protect the kids or Gramps if he planned to use them to hurt her.

He stood, shoving the kids off his lap. They fell to the floor.

Ella cried out, and Carson, bless his heart, moved to shelter her when the sound drew the man's ire. "We're all going for a nice car ride." He used the gun to motion for the kids to walk, nudging Carson's back with the barrel. All the while, his finger grazed the trigger.

One wrong move, one misstep, and her little boy could be—

She gagged. *No, God. Please, God, no.*

"Let's go."

A hot wave crashed over her. Her cheeks, chin, and forehead dampened. Her heart thundered in her ears. The kids held each other, somehow knowing obedience was the only option.

"You too, old man." He nudged Gramps as he reached the recliner.

Gramps pushed off the chair and hobbled behind the kids. He moved like he was unsteady, but Abby glimpsed something in his eyes.

"Don't get any ideas." Devin waved his weapon. "One wrong move and the old man gets it first. Then the kids. Then you."

Abby flinched, but she nodded, feeling for the letter opener in her sleeve. She fell into line behind the others. William would have no one left. He'd suffer like she'd suffered, wondering what he could have done differently, wondering if he'd just come home would the outcome have changed. She didn't want that for him.

Abby couldn't think about that right now. Her muscles tightened in readiness. She had to press forward. The gun poked into her back, and her gut hopscotched. At least now he aimed it at her.

Verses she remembered from her childhood came rushing

back. *Though I walk through the valley of the shadow of death, I fear no evil.*

But she did fear evil. She feared it very much.

You are with me. Your rod and staff, they comfort me.

But they didn't comfort her. She was terrified. She was alone, and if she failed, everyone would die.

Full-body tremors rippled from her head to her toes. If it were just her, she'd manage. She'd faced worse as a police officer, but involving the kids and Gramps, that rained down a whole new level of fear.

Nausea churned. Gramps opened the back door where a van sat with the side door open. If only William had driven around to the back and seen it. If only they had realized it wasn't over. It wasn't even close.

Gramps collapsed against the railing. He leaned on it as he walked down the stairs. Every step pushed out a wheezy breath that grew in volume.

"Hurry, old man." Devin's jerky hands made her chest lurch. His finger was still threaded through the trigger guard. Spittle flew from his mouth.

The fabric of Abby's shirt clung to her back. Once they got into the van, it was all over. Time was running out, and Abby couldn't do anything to turn the tide.

She stumbled. Every second escalated Devin's agitation. Tears blurred her field of vision. She couldn't go without a fight, but a fight would put the kids in the crossfire.

Gramps grabbed his chest and fell to the ground.

The kids screamed.

Abby lurched for Gramps, but Devin jerked her back.

Gramps's body went rigid, his face contorted in agony.

"Get in the van!" Devin screamed.

"Gramps!" Abby reached for him, and the gun went off.

The dirt near Gramps's head puffed and everything stilled except the man rolling and moaning, clasping his chest, struggling to breathe.

The kids' faces paled and their mouths moved, but no words came out. They were in shock. Devin grabbed them by the arms and tossed them toward the vehicle's open side door. Carson's head clubbed against the door frame with a tin-like thump. Ella's lip bled as she scrambled to Carson's side. They huddled in the back of the van, away from the gun, away from the door's opening. Still not making a sound.

Devin lifted his gun. "It's time to say goodbye to Grandpa." He swung to point the gun at Gramps, but he was gone.

The first surge of hope shot through her. *Lord, help Gramps.*

Her phone rang.

Devin froze.

Its familiar tone shrieked through the tension, and she didn't dare reach for it.

"Give it to me." He was infuriated at having been outwitted by an old man, so she didn't dare challenge him. Fire burned in his gaze. He pointed his gun at Ella but kept his eyes on her. "Don't do anything stupid."

She pulled the phone from her pocket with two fingers.

Austin.

She offered it to Devin.

"Toss it in the bushes."

The ringing stopped. The sudden silence cut through her hope. She threw it into the bushes. Austin would know something was wrong when she didn't respond.

"Now get in." He gestured to her.

If she got in, she might never get out. Abby shuffled toward the vehicle until she stood between the open side door and the gun. She blocked the line of fire to the kids with her body. "No."

The phone rang again. *Please, Lord*, was all she could manage.

Would Gramps find help? Would anyone believe the conspiracy theory lover that they were in real danger? What if Gramps wasn't faking? What if that was an actual heart attack, and he'd crawled into the peach orchard to die?

Heat foamed in her body. Her neck and ears burned. She shook her arm and the letter opener in her sleeve slid into her hand. She hid it behind her thigh. It was all up to her now.

"Get in," Devin repeated.

The kids were huddled in the back of the van, but Abby was still outside. She still had a chance to turn this around. She manipulated the letter opener inside her sleeve, hiding it behind her leg. She shuffled closer to the van. Closer to Devin.

"Aren't you worried about the gunshot drawing attention?" Abby curled her fingers around the metal tool. Just a bit closer.

"I've been watching this place. Those bird bangers sound just like a shot. First time I heard it, I hit the dirt," he laughed. It was an awful cackle right out of a cartoon. "Nobody is coming for you."

Ella's wheeziness increased. She was hyperventilating. The girl dragged in a ragged breath. Her chest heaved up and down, and her mouth opened and closed as if she was struggling to gulp in air. The more she tried, the more tense and sweaty she became. Abby kept her attention on Devin and his gun. But she could smell Ella's fear.

"Breathe, Ella," she coaxed, while working to control her

own thudding heart. It slammed against her rib cage, threatening to punch its way free.

Devin was right. The timed bangers that exploded in the orchard kept the birds off the fruit. They sounded just like a gunshot. No one was coming for them. Carson curled into a ball, and Ella, thank the Lord, gained some sort of control.

Devin threw a rope at Abby. It hit her ribs and thudded to the ground. "Tie your hands together."

Abby bent to pick up the twine, and on the downward movement she thrashed out, aiming the blunt instrument for Devin's leg. "Run!" She screamed, spinning from the door.

Devin dodged, but not fast enough. He howled as the blade lacerated his denim and blood streamed down his leg. But it wasn't as deep as Abby had hoped.

Before the kids could escape the van, Devin crammed the barrel against Carson's forehead and leaned in with his body weight. Carson froze, his eyes wide and cross-eyed as they stared at the muzzle pressed against his skin. "Tie yourself up, or he dies."

Abby wound the thick twine around her wrists. "It'll be okay, Carson."

Devin shoved Carson back inside the vehicle and slid the van door closed, trapping the children in the dank and sour back. He stabbed the gun's muzzle between her shoulder blades and cocked the hammer of his weapon. "Do anything like that again, and the kids are dead."

Devin pushed Abby, and she stumbled. He forced her into the front passenger seat.

The musty scent of old food and lingering moisture infiltrated her senses. She had to get him talking. Trick him into making a mistake. Her clumsy attempt to obey frustrated him, and he rewarded her with a slap to the back of her skull.

She fell against the seat's plastic covers. She tasted blood in her mouth. Ringing clouded her thinking, but she registered the lingering smell of alcohol.

As Devin hobbled toward the driver's seat, Abby briefly entertained the idea of locking him out. But if she did, he'd open fire on the vehicle. Only the Lord could help them now.

WILLIAM'S TIRES crunched on the gravel at the shoulder of the road. Few tourists knew about this access point near the beach. At most, he'd see a couple of locals, but the odds were in his favor that he'd be alone, which was exactly what he needed.

A boulder jutted into the water where the Niagara River met Lake Ontario. He'd sat on that rock when his mother died. Again, when his father disappeared. But those times, he'd ridden his bicycle here. This was where Gramps found him when his dad relinquished custody, so William could live with Gramps at the orchard.

William sat on this rock when his wife died after a long battle with cancer, and again when he realized the depths of the financial trouble the fruit farm was in. This was his spot. It's where he came when he needed the Lord.

There was something about the magnitude of a narrow river funneling into a lake that made him feel better. It made it seem possible that a God so much bigger than he could ever imagine had funneled His Spirit into something as small and confined as William's broken and sinful body. This was where the impossible felt possible. He needed that right now. And maybe a miracle. God might as well toss in a bucketful of wisdom while He was at it.

A breeze gathered strength over the water, and William

turned his face toward it. *Lord, what are you doing? I don't understand what is happening or why you're allowing Abby to face such danger. She's come to mean more to me than I realized, and I'm not sure I could survive another loss. Please, Lord, help us.*

William sat quietly. He welcomed the kiss of the wind and the warmth of the sun. The rhythmic lapping of the water on the shore brought Psalm 46 to mind.

God is my refuge and strength, a very present help in trouble.

They certainly had trouble.

I will not fear though the earth gives way, though the mountains be moved into the heart of the sea.

Psalm 46 was a song of confidence meant to be sung. The beach stretched empty for miles, but William wasn't about to sing. He would, however, recite the psalm. Something powerful happened when he spoke God's Word aloud. William began softly, "Though the waters roar and foam, though the mountains tremble at its swelling. Selah."

William had tried to build stable mountains for Ella, but stability had collapsed into the sea years ago. Somewhere along the way, fear clawed into the territory of faith. The storms felt bigger than God. Despite knowing that emotion was an unreliable source of truth, his heart struggled to remember that "There is a river whose streams make glad the city of God."

The figurative river represented the power of God's presence. When everything felt out of control, the river remained under God's power. Its streams made glad... God was here. It didn't matter how much this storm raged, because God was bigger.

Be still and know that I am God.

He was trying.

God was with the Israelites, and Jesus was with him.

Jesus, who calmed another storm and commanded the wind and the waves to be quiet and still, was the same Jesus that promised to never leave or forsake him. Jesus was here, right in the middle of this messed up situation. And even more, He was with Abby, too. He was with every person who confessed His name, and He would not fail them.

So why did it feel like everything was falling apart?

William pulled his knees to his chest and wrapped his arms around them. He didn't expect an audible answer. Usually, what came was a sense of peace, the comforting presence of the Spirit of God. But it didn't come today. Today, his insides crackled like kindling, and he didn't know how to turn the heat down.

The phone in his pocket vibrated against his hip. The unfamiliar number wasn't local. He hit ignore and slipped it back into his pocket.

William inhaled until his lungs filled. His heart continued to throb, and his head remained fuzzy. Peace eluded him.

The phone rang again. Same number. William hit ignore a second time.

If God was his very present refuge, why did his insides surge like the restless and menacing sea?

When his phone rang a third time, he stuffed his frustration down, stabbing the answer button. He growled, "Hello?"

"My name is Austin Emmerson, Abby's former partner. I've been trying to reach her with important, time-sensitive information, but she is not picking up her phone."

William tried to dial back his irritation. There could be a million reasons for Abby not answering the phone. Besides, William didn't know her old partner. Maybe Abby didn't want to speak with him. "She could be busy with Carson."

A huff of irritation.

"I'm not home right now, but I can tell her you called when I return."

"Abby always takes my calls. And if she can't, she sends a text message with a thumbs up, so I know she's okay. It's a system we developed when we worked together."

William's stomach clenched. "Maybe her battery's dead." This came out less confident. Austin was overreacting. He had to be. William swallowed, but the lump in his throat remained. His palms dampened, and he wiped them on his pant legs.

"You don't understand," Austin continued. "Abby's instincts were right. I got sick when she visited. My wife and I. Abby connected our illness to an old case that we worked."

William's chest tingled.

"The felon we put away swore to get revenge. Devin Teale. They released him from prison recently."

William was already off the rock and making his way back to his vehicle. "What makes you think he found Abby?"

"Because he found me."

The pain in the back of his throat intensified.

"If he targeted me while Abby was visiting, then he could have followed Abby to your place. She's not safe."

And he left her alone. William thrust his keys into the ignition but fumbled, and they clattered to the floor. He stabbed the speaker option on the phone and groped around the floor mats for his keychain.

"How did he target you? What did he do?"

"He laced our food with the same street drug we put him away for. It could have killed us if Abby hadn't suggested we screen for that specific toxin."

William's heart picked up pace as he pulled onto the road. The same drug they found in Carson's toy. Gramps had been complaining of worsening stomach pain. Could the guy have laced their food? Was that why Abby had asked Dr. Pike to order more tests on Gramps? Did she suspect poisoning and not tell him? Thoughts piled up like a highway collision, growing bigger by the second. William ran a peach farm. Could all the fruit be tainted? Were his customers in danger? How did they test for something like that?

"Just tell me she's all right."

William's hands tightened on the steering wheel. They'd gone cold and clammy. "I wish I could." He updated Austin on recent events while careening around a corner. As soon as they disconnected, he phoned Abby.

No answer.

William pounded the steering wheel and stabbed redial. *Come on. Pick up.*

Rose was spending the rest of the day with her sister, so she wasn't at the house, and Gramps rarely used his phone, but he tried it anyway. No answer. It probably wasn't turned on. His stomach cramped. His body went icy, choking off his airway. Why did he leave them? Why didn't he check the house before he left?

He zipped up the gravel driveway that led to the main house, spitting stones from his tires. Jethro stopped his work and turned to stare as the trail of dust billowing behind him grew. William thrust the car into park before he'd stopped. It lurched forward and back, throwing him against the strap of the seat belt.

William's gaze glued to the house. He tried Abby's phone again as he got out of the car. A faint ringing sounded. He didn't bother closing the vehicle door. He followed the sound around the side of the house to the back porch. It came from the shrub.

He stuffed his phone in his pocket, keeping the connection open, and rooted around the branches. The image of him with Ella laying her head on his shoulder peeked through the twigs of the bush on an illuminated screen. He threaded his hand through to retrieve Abby's phone. He tapped ignore, and the phone went silent. Fear like he'd never known slammed him. Dread gnawed at his insides. If Abby's phone was here, where were the kids? Gramps? He spun. "Ella? Carson?"

"Everything all right?" Jethro held his sun hat in his hands and looked at William with concern.

Before William could answer, a shuffling sounded from the right. William's hands fisted, and he pulled his right arm back, ready to strike. A roar filled his ears. Fight or flight kicked in, and William knew if he went down, he'd go down swinging.

Gramps staggered from the peach trees, supported by two of their workers. "We found him wandering the rows. He keeps saying we need to call Ella. We shouted for her, but no one came."

Gramps's babbling stopped when he saw William. Scratches marked up Gramps's arms. His wild eyes darted all over. "Willy!" He fell into William's outstretched arms. "He took Abby and the kids!"

Fresh terror reared. "Who took them?"

"I don't know." Gramps was sobbing now. "A man pushed his way into the house. He had a gun." Gramps's entire body shook. He lifted an age-spotted hand to his throat. His shoulders curled, and his spine bent with each raspy breath. "He sat the kids on his lap and waited for Abby. You have to call Ella."

Jethro spoke into his cell phone, probably on the line

with the police. He bounded up the porch stairs and disappeared into the house.

"Ella doesn't have a phone, Gramps." William focused on the two workers who helped Gramps back to the house. "Did you see anything? What kind of car did they leave in?"

"We're working the back quarter today," one worker said.

"It's too far from the house to see," said the other.

William's gut heaved. Guilt over not being there when his family needed him crippled him. He should have been there. He should have inserted himself between the danger and them, but he was off licking his wounds and belly-aching over his hurt feelings.

"I got away," Gramps said. "I pretended to have a heart attack. But I can't remember the phone number."

William helped Gramps onto a porch chair. "There is no phone number, Gramps. Ella doesn't have a phone."

Jethro exited the house with a glass of water and handed it to Gramps. Under his breath, he said, "I looked around. No one is here. The police are on their way."

William bounced Abby's phone against his thigh. Think. The police were on their way to the house to speak with Gramps, but if Austin was right and this Devin man had Abby and the children, every second counted.

"You're not listening to me." Gramps pounded his fist on his thigh.

Everybody froze at the outburst.

"Ella has MY phone. I can't remember the number."

William's heart jolted. "Your phone?"

"I slipped it into her pocket when no one was looking."

Good old Gramps! William dialed the number. Hope crashed when the automated answering service came on. "Was the phone turned on, Gramps?"

He nodded. "Yes, but I turned the sound off."

Jethro slipped an arm around Gramps's shoulder and squeezed. "It was smart to give her the phone."

William said, "Abby might not have time to wait for the police." Abby's lock screen required a password. If he could break into her phone, he might be able to track her through her fitness watch. It uploaded data to the corresponding app. He inputted Carson's birthday. No luck.

Abby's resume had dates. He fumbled for his cell and accessed the file, checking the dates of her past work experience. He tried the date she started on the police force. Nope. The date she left the police force. Incorrect again. Six failed attempts and the phone locked him out for a minute.

"Gramps, do you have any idea what Abby's passcode might be?" Gramps's gaze followed William as William paced back and forth on the porch. Jethro had pulled over a chair beside Gramps, and he patted his knee.

Gramps lifted a shaky hand to his temple. "Passcode?" he echoed, wrinkling his forehead.

William dragged a hand through his hair. Gramps's clarity was fading. The phone notified William that the minute was up and he could try again. His fingers hovered over the keypad. If he failed again, the phone would lock him out for five minutes. He tried the date Abby started working for him. Wrong again.

William flung open the house door and hurried inside. "I'm searching her room for a clue. If I'm wrong again, it'll lock me out for fifteen minutes."

And Abby might not have fifteen minutes.

Jethro helped Gramps to his feet, who hobbled after William. Abby's room was painted in sunset hues. The sunset faded with each wall, making it look as if the room were getting darker. A large wooden bed shared a wall with a tall nightstand and a chest of drawers. There were two windows with red drapes drawn. A window seat below one window and a book rested on the cushion.

William flipped through Abby's book, and Jethro aided Gramps to the bed before he began searching the drawers. "What are we looking for?" Jethro asked.

William pulled the drawers from the tall chest. How on earth were they supposed to deduce a four-digit code? As a cop, she'd know not to pick something easily identifiable. "Any four-digit number of significance to Abby."

"What about this?" Jethro held up a banner from a road race. Stamped on the front of the bib was the number Abby would have worn as a runner.

The phone buzzed with a notification that William could try again. Gramps snorted and his nostrils flared. His face reddened. Lord, sustain Gramps. Give him the strength to endure. William wouldn't be able to manage if Gramps went down.

"If Abby saved the bib, maybe it was an important race."

William roared, making Gramps jump. *A little help here, God!* "Where did you find it?" William asked Jethro.

"In here." Jethro stepped aside so William could look in the box he'd sat on the bed. Memorabilia from road races, half-marathons, 5k fun runs and medals galore. The passcode could be any of these bib numbers. Wait. Most of the medals were participant medals. But one was first-place. William picked it up and turned it over. A run supporting a women's shelter. On the back of the medal was the shelter name and the year. It was earlier this year.

William pulled up the race information on his phone.

After a few more minutes of searching, he found the times for the runners. Abby's race time was 21:04.

His hand shook. *Please, Lord.* He inputted the digits 2, 1, 0, 4. "It worked!"

"Good boy, Willy." Gramps grinned.

William's fingers slid over the screen. "Abby has a fitness watch, and it's connected to her phone. I can trace her location through that." A couple more swipes, and he had it. Knots tightened in his gut. Horseshoe Falls.

"What should we do?" Jethro asked.

"The police are on their way." William tucked Abby's phone into his back pocket and grabbed a paper and pen from the small writing desk. "Tell them I went to this location, the place her watch is." He pressed the paper into Jethro's palm. William paused by Gramps and looked into his eyes. The man appeared lucid again, but the disease showed up at strange times. By the time the police arrived, Gramps could be trapped in another memory. "Are you good, Gramps?"

Gramps squeezed William's upper arm and held William's gaze. "Go get our family."

"I'll stay with him," Jethro promised. "And make sure they know Ella has Robert's phone."

William nodded. Tremors started in his hands and ran up his forearms until his entire body quaked. They were gone, and their only witness was a man with an unreliable memory, suffering from dementia. Where was God? Where was His very present help as this mountain fell into the sea?

THIRTEEN

Abby expected Devin to take them into the woods and off them somewhere secluded, but he pointed the gun at her with one hand and steered the vehicle with the other. They sped away from Chenaniah River.

The country road was hard and jagged against the growling tires. Crushed nuts and fallen leaves sprayed behind them. Nobody traveled these roads unless they were coming to the farm. They wouldn't pass anyone. Sweat dampened Abby's armpits as the shadows cast from the trees shaded them. Everything was green from a recent rainfall. Sunlight jumped off the hood whenever it broke through the trees.

"Your attempt to poison Austin didn't work." She hoped to distract him long enough to give her an opportunity to act. She pulled at the rope binding her hands. He hadn't checked how well she'd bound them.

He scoffed. "You can't imagine how lucky I felt when I

saw you and your boy sitting at your old partner's dining room table. He was easy to locate. You had proven more difficult after you left the force."

If she could keep him talking, that would give the others more time to find them. Gramps got away. Gramps would get help. He had to. As she loosened the ropes, she tried to camouflage her movement by adjusting her position on the seat. Her pulse escalated. It sounded like a staccato drum beating in her skull. It became a haunting song, and the more she inhaled and exhaled, the more her rope-burned wrists throbbed. Her gaze darted to the children, who huddled together, whimpering.

Fear for them swelled, and she battled for composure. "Austin is going to be fine. Your plan failed."

His only reaction was cutting his eyes toward her and flexing his hand on the steering wheel.

"I figured it out. I told him to get a tox screen specific to the drug you made. He'd have the results by now. They'll be treating him accordingly."

Devin's upper lip curled. "I can circle back to him. Today is all about you. You and your kids."

He thought Ella was hers as well. Poor William, getting dragged into her mess after already suffering so much loss.

"You think you're so smart. You think you've got it all figured out." Devin continued, as if he needed to get this off his chest. "But you didn't even recognize me at the rest stop. You don't deserve to be a parent. You don't deserve them." He jerked his head toward the back, where the kids were. "You deserve to cry and plead and beg." A sinister smile curved his lips. "And you will."

She ran her tongue over her lips. Abby wasn't afraid for herself, just the kids. She could hear them rolling around with each jerk of the steering wheel, not having a car seat to keep them safe.

"I was going to kill you, but after some thought, I decided a more fitting punishment was to let you live."

She stilled as they merged onto the highway.

"That's right." He cackled. "You'll live, but it'll be torture. You'll spend the rest of your life knowing someone took your children from you, just like you took mine."

The boulder in Abby's throat grew to a size that made it impossible to speak. Dozens of cars sped past them. If someone looked her way, if they saw her —

It was like he could read her mind. "Don't get any ideas. If anyone interferes, I'll kill you. Right in front of your kids. And I'll still keep your kids."

She turned her face away from the window. Vehicles sped past them, oblivious to their agony.

Only an occasional sniff from the back broke the silence. Finally, the van exited the highway. After another fifteen minutes, Devin slammed on the brakes. The van skidded sideways, and the kids screamed. Abby shut her eyes. The river roared like a dragon. It only raged like this at the rapids above Horseshoe Falls. William had taken them there one afternoon for a picnic. *Lord, help us.*

Abby locked gazes with Devin. He sneered. There was no talking Devin off the ledge. She felt it in her gut. "I only need one of your kids alive to make this punishment fitting. You try anything, and the girl gets it right between the eyes." Devin looked in the back. "Get up here," he growled, motioning to Ella.

Ella shrank and shook her head. She scrambled behind Carson, who puffed his chest out and stared at Devin in defiance.

Devin reached into the rear and clamped onto Carson's arm. He yanked him up between the front seats and pushed the gun against his temple. "I don't care who I kill first. Get out of the car."

Abby's hands shook as she opened the passenger door. Devin pulled Carson between the seats into the front. They exited through the driver's door.

"Get the girl."

Abby slid the side door open, her hands still bound, and forced a smile. Ella had crawled all the way into the back and covered her ears with her hands. When Ella's eyes met hers, she said, "I want my daddy."

"I do, too, Sweetheart." Abby choked on her words, realizing how much she meant them. If William lost Ella, he'd never forgive her.

"Hurry!" Devin shoved her.

"I'm trying." She refocused on Ella. "Come to me, Sweetheart. I need you to come to me so the bad man doesn't hurt Carson."

Ella crawled out so slowly that Abby feared Devin might shoot Carson just to hurry her obedience.

"Why are you doing this?" Abby asked as she helped Ella out. The girl cowered behind Abby's legs.

"You need to know what it feels like to have someone more powerful than you take your kids away."

"I didn't take your kids. You lost them. You and their mom went to jail. What did you expect would happen?"

Devin released Carson and grabbed her by the hair. He dragged her toward the water's edge, where a boat bobbed against a dock. He yelled over his shoulder for the kids to keep up or he'd shoot her. Droplets of water hit her skin like a thousand arrow pricks. They were about a mile from the brink of the falls. Waves tumbled with the screech of an over-strung guitar, taut and vibrating on the verge of snapping.

There was a motor on the boat attached to the dock, so Devin could navigate anywhere.

"When I got out of jail, no one would tell me where my kids were. Now, you'll live the rest of your life not knowing where your kids are."

He threw her to the ground. Abby's mouth filled with dirt.

"Did he keep them?" he growled. "Did he sell them? Is someone hurting them? Every day for the rest of your life will be a nightmare of not knowing."

Abby lifted her face in time to see him toss the children into the dinghy. Carson's lips formed a perfect oval. His eyes blinked and glistened with tears. "Mommy!"

"Put on the life jackets," Abby said as she crawled toward the craft. Not that life jackets would help. If they landed in the water, the falls would take them.

They fumbled with the jackets under the seat, the clasps proving to be more difficult than they could manage. Abby wanted to help them, but she couldn't see. Her eyes were bleary and unfocused. But she'd worked her hands free from the ropes. She held them together as if they were still bound.

With his gun trained on Abby, Devin boarded the rocking vessel. When she started to follow, he cocked his weapon. "Not so fast."

He moved like he was about to push the boat from the shore. A lowlife like Devin had a million ways to disappear. They were near the border. He could go anywhere. Abby would never find the kids if he got away.

She waited until he turned to the motor. It was the tiniest movement. She lunged onto the boat.

Abby wrapped her hands around the gun's muzzle. She wrenched it away from the kids. The boat rocked. Carson and Ella gripped the edge, screaming. Water lapped inside and pooled at their feet. She had to get the gun. She had to save the kids.

The gun fired.

The blast was deafening. For a moment, everyone went quiet. All she could smell was powder, oil, and sweat. Abby staggered. Her vision blurred. Her shoulder burned. "No," she slurred.

The children's screams faded as if someone had turned the volume down. Abby fell into the water. Fighting to maintain consciousness, she wouldn't go gently. She'd kick and scream the entire way.

Devin chuckled. He dropped his arm to his side and laughed. "Maybe you'll die today, after all." He fired up the boat's motor and left her in the wake.

Abby's breath came in quick gasps. The current snagged her and dragged her away from the shore. She could barely make out the blurred landscape. Her mind slowed, and her limbs grew heavy, but her eyes remained wide open. She gagged as a wave slapped her cheek. She could see the cliff face on the other side of the river. It wouldn't be long before she hit the falls. She squinted and saw the spray, a huge rainbow feathering over the edge and the water roared like a train.

WILLIAM ARRIVED AT HORSESHOE FALLS, the largest of the three falls that formed the Niagara River. He sprinted along a path that led to the water's edge. This wasn't the populated side of the falls where all the tourists gathered to marvel at the wonder of God's creation. William approached from the back. Abby was at the part of the river that fed into the falls, the spot the locals knew enough to avoid. The phone showed her as being on or near the water. *Lord, please keep them safe.*

The smell of damp earth and plant life thickened the air. William swatted tree branches as he ran. Off in the distance, he could make out a small grouping of people. Two adults and two children huddled in a boat bobbing the waves. *Thank you, Lor—*

A blast exploded. One figure plummeted into the river.

"Nooooo!" Adrenaline rushed through William. Everything tunneled to the scene unfolding. The powerful downward current snatched Abby and pulled her under.

Alerted by his cry, the second figure faced William, pointed a gun, and fired again.

William hit the ground.

A bullet thudded into the trunk of a nearby tree.

From this angle, William spied an abandoned canoe, flipped upside down and propped on a tree stump. No one canoed at Horseshoe Falls. You needed a motor to fight the current, and even with one, no one boated at the top of the falls. But the homeless community often dragged odd items into the trees and repurposed them for shelter.

William scrambled toward the boat. He flipped it and dragged it to the water. The rapids had already pulled Abby's body away.

An oar waited like a gift from the hand of God at the edge. William's paddling added to the water's powerful pull, and it helped close the distance between him and Abby. A motor boat roared on the far side of the river. He could hear the kids screaming his name over the crash of the rapids. The churn of the water and the roar of the waterfall forced his decision. If he went for the children, Abby would die. The kids still had a chance if the police could ping Gramps's phone.

William maneuvered alongside Abby. She fought to keep her head above water. She grabbed the edge of the canoe. "Get the kids," she screamed. Her fingers slipped, and a wave rolled over her head. The current pulled them closer and closer to the edge of the waterfall. They had only seconds.

"Trust me." William fumbled for a grip on her, but the water pulled her away. Her body brushed against his hand. His fingers went numb, and his back ached as he fought for a hold.

Abby slapped him away. "The kids. The kids." She gulped mouthfuls of water, gagging. Her head slipped under the surface. The choppy water churned red with her blood.

Every person Abby had ever depended on let her down. William knew that. He didn't want to be another name on that list. He looked in the direction the boat with the children had gone. It was too late. They were only dots on the horizon. He turned back to Abby, but she was gone. For one horrible second, William thought the falls had taken her until her body rose with the swell of a wave. She had stopped fighting.

"No!" The raging water swallowed his cry. His heart thrashed in his chest. He maneuvered the canoe alongside her again and grabbed onto a limb. He heaved. The canoe rocked precariously. They were still tracking toward the falls. He heaved again.

Hundreds of tourists mulled near the railings. Someone noticed them and screamed. Soon, people were shouting and gesturing.

The canoe flipped. Water splashed his face. He came up gasping. His chest felt like it was about to explode. The water's roar distorted screaming from the shoreline. The throngs pointed ahead. Then he saw it. The Iron Scow.

In 1918, the barge-like vessel lodged in the shallow rapids above the falls. If he could direct them there, it might be enough to save them.

A rush pulled him under. The water threw Abby's limp body against him. He grabbed on and pulled her to his chest. He kicked to the surface. His muscles strained under Abby's dead weight. He wasn't going to make it. Dots exploded behind his eyes. Her body dragged like weights. He threaded his arm through the back of her shirt, from hem to collar, to free both his hands. The water roiled around him. A rope from the canoe brushed against his arm. William grabbed on. It cut into his flesh, but he held firm. The canoe, powered by the current, dragged him downstream.

His fingers were numb. Cold bit at the tips of his fingers while blood stung his mouth. Red colored the water, but he didn't know if it was his or Abby's blood. White froth filled his vision. Water cascaded over Abby's face. Her skin gray. Eyes closed.

The canoe hit the barge with enough force to crack it in two. As the boat split apart, William released the rope. The water thrust them against the Iron Scow. William turned and absorbed the hit. Pain jolted him. He hit the side and slipped beneath the surface of the water, pulling Abby with him. Throbbing darkened his vision. He tried to hold on to Abby. His body skimmed across a rough surface. He grabbed hold with one hand and crawled onto the wooden barge, his grip slipping. Water splashed his face, filling his eyes and burning his nose. He dragged Abby behind him. She wasn't moving. The crowd on the shoreline cheered.

The pieces of the canoe disappeared over the foaming

edge of the water. They'd been so close to death. His body, numbed by the chill, groaned, echoing the deep reverberation in the barge's belly. Everything blurred. William's cheek rested against the rough wood. The coppery tang of blood filled his mouth. The waves crashed at their feet, but he had nothing left. His eyes shut. He just wanted the pain to stop.

FOURTEEN

bby's lips cracked. They hurt, but she couldn't remember why. She turned her head. Stiffness scratched her cheek. She puckered, not smelling the familiar scent of her fabric softener. Disinfectant replaced it. It tasted—she dampened her lips—sterile and cold.

The air moved, and tendrils of hair tickled her neck. She should brush them back, but her arms felt like dead weights. She was too tired to care. It was easier to drift. It was almost enjoyable to ride the gentle current, tugging her back toward darkness, warmth, and hazy weightlessness.

Heaviness covered her hand. Pressure squeezed it. It pulled her toward the light. She squeezed her eyes tighter, and pain zipped across her forehead. She frowned.

"Abby, it's time to wake up."

The husky voice gently commanded her. Something about it made her insides hum. He was safe. She could trust him. She felt it deep in her bones.

"Abby?"

She tried to peel open her eyes, but a crusty film glued them together. The warmth left her hand and moved to her eyelids, pressing softly. Dampness gently wiped away the stickiness.

"Try again, Sweetheart. Open your eyes for me."

Sweetheart?

She was so tired. Why wouldn't he let her sleep?

"Abby?"

No longer inviting, the voice grated on her. Abby groaned and inhaled deeply. Painful fireworks exploded behind her lids. She squeezed her eyes closed. It hurt. She wanted to drift. To not feel. Just for a few more blessed minutes. Every cell in her body was so heavy.

A rustle. Then, a flutter caressed her cheek. "Mommy?" Little fingers poked her.

Carson.

Her eyes snapped open. Everything rushed back in a tidal wave. Devin forcing the kids onto a boat. Fighting for the gun. Blinding hot pain and churning water. Then William was there.

Like he was right now.

William cradled Carson with one hand and held her hand with his other. Carson leaned as far forward as he could without toppling out of William's arms and poked her again. "You sleeped a really long time."

His stretched eyes and pouty lips told her what he thought about her extended rest. She laughed. At least she tried to laugh, but it came out like a soft moan.

She dragged her gaze over her baby, noting every limb and feature, and the absence of bandages and visible bruises. He looked perfect. A wave of gratitude was followed by fear. "Ella?"

She snapped her gaze to William. Dampness coated her cheeks. Her heart caught.

"Everybody's safe." William squeezed her hand again.

The weight compressing her chest lifted.

"She's in the hall. They only let a few of us in at a time."

A few of us? Who was out there?

Abby tried to push herself up. Medical equipment whirred to the right, emitting the occasional beep. Sunlight poured in the window. Cool bedding tucked under her back. Her non- IV hand was warm, still in William's grip. "You got the kids. How?"

William set Carson on the side of the bed, being careful not to disturb her intravenous line. He helped her into a sitting position, and Carson snuggled into the crook of her uninjured arm. Pain shot through her shoulder. A huge white bandage covered most of the square footage of her upper body.

Devin shot her. Wooziness distorted William's face. Shot. A bullet. The very reason she left the police force. She was supposed to do better. She was supposed to be safe working as a personal support worker, and she got shot anyway.

William lifted a nearby plastic cup and slipped the straw between her lips. "Have a drink."

She sipped. Tepid water soothed the rawness inside.

"Good girl," he said, nodding.

"I wanna help. Drink more." Carson pushed the cup to her lips again.

When William seemed satisfied she wasn't about to faint, he set the cup back down. He lifted a piece of ice and held it to her lips. "Open."

When his fingertips brushed her mouth, a tingle swept

through her. She sucked on the ice chip, the cold providing unexpected relief.

"The police caught Devin upstream. Gramps sent them after him. I came for you."

"Gramps is okay?" Her heart squeezed. How could she have forgotten about Gramps? He'd collapsed, clutching his chest, writhing in pain. Then he was gone.

William chuckled and an odd smile twisted his lips. "More than okay. Remember that tracking device we found on Carson?"

She nodded. The movement made her head swim. She squeezed her eyes shut.

"No sleep again. Mommy stays awake now." Carson patted her.

She forced her eyes open, and Carson's stern expression made her heart flip-flop.

"It gave Gramps an idea. He planted his phone on Ella. He didn't know how to track it, but figured the police could."

New morning mercies. Thank you, Lord.

A man in a stiff white jacket poked his head into the room. "I hear somebody's awake?"

She smiled and winced.

The doctor's tanned skin was warm, his eyes kind, and his mannerisms were full of compassion. "I'm Dr. Smith. I've been taking care of you. You took a nasty hit to the jaw. Nothing's broken, but it's a pretty bad bone bruise." He made a note on her chart. "The bullet was a through-and-through. Nothing major was hit, but it'll be sore for a while. You're lucky."

She nodded. She'd been shot. It felt surreal.

"Let me look at your vitals, and if everything checks out like I expect it to, we'll let that family of yours in to see you."

"My family?" Her parents were dead. Her only living and breathing relative was the boy tucked in beside her.

William reached for Carson, who went to him willingly. They tracked every move the doctor made as if she were still in danger. Carson's concerning frown would have made Abby giggle if every muscle in her body wasn't already screaming in pain.

"They're a pretty rowdy bunch." Dr. Smith continued on about her family, chuckling as he listened to her heart and checked the numbers on the machine hooked up to her. His fingers felt like ice cubes against her skin. "But they love you. That's clear."

Abby's head spun.

Dr. Smith's eyes softened as he watched her process the information. He didn't hurry. Didn't press. Just waited for her brain to catch up. "It all looks good." He patted her leg.

The words were hardly out of his mouth when the door swung open and Rose hurried in, holding Ella's hand. Gramps hobbled behind her, supported by a man she didn't recognize but who had similar features to William. Austin and Sandy caboosed. Her family.

The stranger helped Gramps into a chair, then came to stand beside William. Up close, the similarities were even clearer. Same square jawline. Same narrow nose and prominent forehead. Like father and son.

Father and son!

"Are you?" She didn't finish. She didn't have to.

He extended his hand. "I'm Michael, William's dad. We didn't get the chance to speak, but the message you left put all this into motion."

"But how?" She didn't know if her muddled thoughts were from the painkillers pumping through the IV, the whack she took on her head, or the unbelievable twist standing in front of her.

"After you left Dad a message, he tried calling you back. When he couldn't get through, he came home. Said you convinced him." William's eyes shone with dampness. He wasn't angry with her for interfering. He was grateful?

But how did she convince Michael? There were too many missing pieces in this puzzle. It made her head thick and tired.

Michael's warm eyes stayed on hers. "I thought I was saving William from hurt by staying away. I'd convinced myself I didn't deserve his love. But I've been sober for seven years, and I might not deserve forgiveness, but William deserved to hear me request it."

Her eyes found William's. Earlier, he was mad when she poked into his history. Her heart beat faster. What changed?

"Dad called after the ambulance brought you in. I had nothing but time while I waited for an update, which ended up being just enough time to hear Dad's story."

Michael picked up the narrative. "After you reached out, and I couldn't get ahold of you, I grew concerned. Yes, Gramps was sometimes very creative in how he balanced the books," Michael said, flicking a look at his father. "But it wasn't anything shady. He shifted numbers around to make things look less desperate than they were, mostly so Mom wouldn't worry. The government always got every penny they were owed. And once he won custody of William, he stopped even that. The farm relied heavily on its line of credit before harvest, but it usually landed in the black after. So I knew whatever was happening now had nothing to do with him."

It wasn't connected to Gramps because she brought the

trouble with her. Her chin trembled. "It's my fault. I'm so sorry, William. When I put Devin away, he lost his kids. He wanted revenge."

"That's not 100 percent accurate," Austin interrupted. He stepped to the foot of the bed and squeezed her toes. She'd forgotten he and Sandy were there. They'd stood in the back, letting the others have her attention. That was so often their way. Quietly serving. Putting others first. Waiting with patience.

"When I got here, I drilled the Roths hard. Something didn't add up. Devin followed you from my place and tormented you for fun, but it wasn't until Joe cracked that it started to make sense. He confessed to tormenting you with threatening notes, trying to get you to leave and setting the cottage on fire."

Her sharp intake threw her into a coughing fit that raked razors through her wounds. She hadn't noticed Joe's absence until now. How could he do something so awful? They could have died!

"All those threatening notes were from Uncle Joe?"

William lifted the water to her lips again. She sipped, and the coughing spasm stopped. William returned the cup to the side table and picked up her hand, re-anchoring her. "Joe believed the cottage was still empty."

"And for what it's worth, I believe him," Austin added.

"But the worst was Joe's admission to giving Gramps cyanide made from peach pits," William said.

"Micro-doses from peach-pit extract," Austin explained. "Enough to cause GI distress and confusion but not lethal."

"So it looked like cognitive decline," Abby finished.

"My own boy." Gramps wiped his eyes.

"Why?" she asked. It came out all rough and low. Scratchy.

"He figured if you left and Gramps was unwell, he'd have to go into a care facility. The orchard would sell, and his cut would—"

"—pay off his gambling debts," Abby said. She looked at Austin and Sandy. "And you guys? You're okay?"

Sandy's gaze filled with such motherly tenderness that Abby's insides swelled. "Your hunch about the drugs was right. As soon as we got onto the right treatment, we healed up quickly."

She frowned. That didn't add up. "You couldn't have had time for treatment and gotten here this quickly."

"Abby," William waited until she looked at him, "it's been three days since they pulled us from the river."

Three days? Her heart skipped. Who took care of Carson? Who made sure he was safe and wasn't scared?

"You were pretty banged up. That shoulder needed surgery, and your body needed to recover." William bent down until he was at eye level with her. He held her gaze until her mind stopped spinning. "I had Carson. I will always take care of Carson."

Her eyes brimmed. A sense of peace she'd never known filled her.

"Me and Ella played." Carson leaned out of William's arms. He situated Carson back at her side, where he nuzzled into the curve of her neck. "We played horses, walked the doggie, and Gramps taught me checkers." Carson shifted and pressed both palms against her cheeks and looked right into her eyes. They could have bumped noses if she had leaned forward. "Wanna play checkers? I teach you."

William scooped him up again, flipped him over in his

arms, and tickled his belly. "Let's let Mommy rest some more. You'll have lots of time to teach her after she comes home."

Home.

The word warmed the place in her soul that had been cold for too many winters. Her heart had been stuck, forgetting the promise of summer and new morning mercies.

Carson giggled.

Clarity shot through Abby with more force than the bullet. She had what she's always wanted, what she thought had eluded her for her entire life: community, family, and friends.

Gramps fought his muddled mind to get help. Austin and Sandy showed up in more ways than one. William followed her into the storm and saved her from the edge of the falls. The weight she'd carried for her entire adult life lifted. She might be a single mom, but she didn't have to be alone.

She had a family.

PRESSURE BUILT inside William's chest as Abby snuggled Carson and chatted with Austin. His heart thumped and his cheeks warmed. The kindness of the Lord overwhelmed him. Abby was going to be okay.

"What I don't understand is why Devin put the drugs in Carson's bear," Sandy said. "He didn't need to do that. He could have tormented you without the extra hassle."

"I think I know." Abby recalled the police officer who waved at Carson. The one she followed outside because Devin had given her the creeps. "There was an officer at the rest stop. If Devin was afraid he'd get made, stashing the drugs on a kid is perfect. No one would ever look there."

"But then he needed them back," Austin added. "He was

cooking for a big-name guy, and shorting the delivery would be suicide."

"That's why he broke into the cottage to look for them, tried to get into the main house, and tampered with my car."

"It's also why he was at the hospital and why he put that tracker on Carson." William was concerned the information was too much, but Abby kept pulling for more. It was like she needed to know why.

"But after he got the drugs back?" She didn't finish her question.

Austin exchanged a look with Sandy. "After was just for fun. I wish we had made the connection to him sooner."

"A warped and twisted sort of fun," William muttered.

"I've been helping Officer Andy Reuben put the pieces together," Austin said. "He's going to want to speak with you now that you're awake."

Abby just nodded. "And Uncle Joe? He did everything else?"

William got her confusion. It was a lot to wrap the mind around, and the rest of them had spent three days wading through the mess. "Uncle Joe was in deep with some bad guys. He owed a significant amount of money. When he was managing the orchard, he could make payments. But when I took over, his access to the money stopped. To put on the pressure, they threatened Gramps. They were in the orchard when Gramps was lost, in the house the day Uncle Joe fell down the stairs, and it was them at the carnival."

"Why would they shoot Isabelle?"

"She'd started poking into the family and uncovered Joe's debt. It wouldn't have taken her long to connect it to them. They needed to quiet her."

"I think it's time to draw this party to a close." Dr. Smith frowned as he scanned the room. "I know you've waited a long time to see her, but she needs her rest. I don't want exhaustion to cause a setback."

The others nodded, murmuring yes, of course, and started the goodbyes. But William wasn't ready yet. He needed to tell Abby everything that had happened—how the kids had rebounded, and the doctors assured him they'd be okay, how his dad fit seamlessly into their family again and it filled him with gratitude. But mostly, he wanted to tell her how much he loved her.

His mouth flooded with moisture, and he swallowed. Still, his throat felt raw. His ears buzzed. If he said any of those things, if he put it all out there and she wasn't ready, he could ruin whatever this was that had started between them. What if she didn't feel the same way?

Abby's cheeks flushed, and her voice quivered. "Can you stay?"

She was looking at him. Every muscle lost tension. William nodded.

His dad extended his hand to Carson but looked at Abby for permission. "May I?"

"If Carson will go with you, yes."

Michael's eyes softened, and an overwhelming lightness filled William's chest as his dad walked out the door, one hand filled with Carson and the other with Ella. Abby had given him so much. If not for her, he wouldn't have reconnected with his dad. Ella wouldn't have a grandfather. Gramps wouldn't have his son back. They wouldn't be a complete family.

Gramps cleared his throat. "Rose and I will take care of dinner. Austin, would you and Sandy like to stay a few more days at the main house? Then you can have some more time with Abby tomorrow?"

"We'd love that." Sandy's eyes brightened.

"They've been staying with us?" Abby's eyebrows lifted and she fanned her fingers across her breastbone.

Us. Dampness tingled on the back of William's neck. Somehow, amid all that transpired, they'd become us.

"Of course they are." William grasped her hand. Her skin was pale, circles under her eyes hung like bruises. Her hair was limp and bedraggled, her lips dry and cracked, but she'd never looked more beautiful. "That's what family does."

Her cheeks glowed. She took a large, deep, savoring breath, and then smiled. She smiled wider than her bruised jaw should have allowed.

All William knew was that he wanted to be the one to put that look of satisfaction and joy on her face forever. The sounds of the hospital played like a background symphony of beeps, clicks, and buzzing. His heart throbbed with a steady thumping. He had two days to work through all that had happened, and it still felt surreal.

"I'm going to hang around a bit longer." William pulled a chair closer to the bed as the others filed out.

Austin held his gaze for a moment and then lifted his chin. "You take care of her. She made it through her entire career on the force without getting shot."

Sandy slapped him on the arm. "It's too soon to joke about it!" Soft chuckles followed them out the door as it whooshed closed behind them.

William leaned across Abby's bed and held her hand in his. His skin tingled at the sensation. Now it was just the two of them. The words he'd been scripting for the last three days got all tangled up. How did a man go about confessing his love for the woman he employed? Could he? This had to be some sort of human resources violation. But while she lay in the hospital unconscious, he'd done a lot of talking with God. He learned a few things that he could no longer deny. He loved Abby Sinclair, and he wanted to spend the rest of his life showing her how much she meant to him.

The thin hospital sheets felt rough against his arm and they stretched over Abby as an unwelcome reminder of her injuries. William finally lifted his gaze and found her watching him. The corners of her lips twitched. "You are amazing," she said.

"Me?" he squawked. He actually squawked like a prepubescent boy in that awkward stage of adolescence.

She rubbed her thumb over his hand. The soft caress was as gentle and tender as the brush of lips. "You saved me. How can I ever thank you?"

"You saved me," he countered. "I haven't lived—really lived—since Claire died. I haven't loved," he stumbled. He had to say it. Even if she turned him down, it wouldn't change the fact that she had changed him for the better. "I'm falling in love with you, Abby. You and Carson. It's like my puzzle was incomplete until now."

A single tear rolled down her cheek. Great, he made her cry. He leaned closer and used his thumb pad to wipe it away.

She wrapped her palm around his hand. "At police college, they taught us that a heightened sense of danger can spur intense feelings."

Her words splashed a bucket of cold water on his heart. "No." He shook his head. He wouldn't accept it. It felt too real to be anything but real.

"Your feelings might dim with time."

He released her hand. Was she trying to let him down easily? Was this her way of saying that she planned to move on?

Her skin flushed. She rolled her lip into her mouth, and the way she bit down made him smile. No, she was protecting herself from hope. She was afraid of loving him. She was afraid it might not last.

"I did not forge this feeling in danger." His certainty grew with each word. "I love the way you look at Ella. How you care for Gramps. How you laugh at all my lame jokes. I love how comfortable you are discussing the Bible and your doubts and fears with me. I love that you are real. This is real."

He wanted to be there for Abby and fulfill all the ways she'd been longing for family. He wanted to show her that she mattered. That their love could last. That he wasn't walking away. He'd known for some time this was how he felt. He tried to ignore it and pretend it wasn't real. He tried to convince himself that she needed better than him. But he couldn't.

He hadn't been looking for love. In fact, he never thought he'd love again. But here he was. In love. 100 percent. No going back.

He stared into her green eyes, memorizing them. The way they filled told him what her words couldn't.

She loved him. She just didn't know it yet.

"We belong together," he said. "Call it a God-thing, call it whatever you want, but I believe He brought you to me to meet a need I didn't know I had."

She released a breath in a rush. It told him all the things she wasn't saying. No matter what the future held, they'd face it together.

Her fingers reached for his. They wrapped around his hand, and she finally said the words he wanted to hear so badly that it hurt. "I love you, too."

Just like that, all the hard places inside of him softened. She loved him. She loved him!

Images of their future filled his mind. Soft blankets. Roaring fires. Hot coffee. Ella and Carson on the carpet playing with Dreyfuss. Gramps and Dad and Rose filling the house with laughter. The main house would not be quiet any longer. No more empty rooms. No more echoes of loneliness. This love was for real. It was the kind that filled the voids until they overflowed. It was built on friendship and respect. A common faith. Shared goals.

"It's going to be difficult for the orchard to rebound financially. We are in for some tight years, but Jethro thinks we can do it. If we're careful, if we plan a modest wedding—"

He hadn't meant to say that. It was too soon to talk about marriage. But she looked up at him, eyes wide and beautiful. Lips soft and inviting.

Maybe it wasn't too soon. He stroked his fingertips against her cheek.

"About that," she said.

"About a wedding?"

"About the money." Her tongue ran over her upper lip. After a second, she spoke. "I never told you this, but my parents left me an inheritance. I'll receive it on my thirtieth birthday."

"But that's yours," he started.

She pressed a finger to his lips. "Ours. And I'm sure the bank will float you enough to carry the farm until then. The orchard will be just fine."

"Kiss her already!" Gramps had poked his head into the room and watched from the doorway.

Abby's cheeks flushed. Her pupils dilated. "You heard the man." The tiniest smile softened her face. She lifted her chin and extended her neck. It was all the invitation he needed.

He leaned in. The side of his bristly cheek grazed her soft one. Her warm breath mixed with his. He hesitated. Their first kiss was going to be witnessed by Gramps and the kids. By Austin, and Sandy, and Rose. They all crowded around the door.

She lifted her face.

His breath quickened. He didn't care who watched. He pressed his lips to hers. The cheers erupting from the hallway had nothing on the fireworks exploding in his soul.

They were home.

FIFTEEN

CHRISTMAS

S now drifted in lazy spirals over the orchard, softening the bare peach trees with a dusting of white. Abby tightened Carson's scarf and tugged his hat lower over his ears, laughing when he wriggled impatiently.

"Hold still, or you'll be frozen solid before we even get to the house."

"Gramps said if we're late, he'll open all the stockings by himself," Carson declared with wide-eyed urgency, puffing white mist into the air.

"Did he now?" Abby shook her head, smiling. "Well, we can't let that happen."

She glanced around the cottage before closing the door behind them. It was small, cozy, and worn in all the right ways. After William had the cottage repaired, she and Carson moved in. And though she spent most of her days in the main house caring for Gramps, she cherished returning here with Carson at night. Having their own space gave her room to breathe while she and William figured out their future together.

As they walked the short path between the cottage and the big house, her flashlight cast golden circles across the snow. The smell of turkey and cinnamon wafted even outside, and the hum of voices carried through the frosted windows.

When Carson pushed the door open, warmth and light banished the winter chill.

"About time!" Gramps called from his armchair near the fire. His cheeks were flushed with life and his eyes twinkled as Carson ran into his arms. "I thought I'd have to start the Christmas Eve stockings without you two stragglers."

Abby helped Carson out of his coat and her heart swelled at the sight. A few months ago, she never would have imagined Gramps looking so strong and mischievous. But his mind was sharper than ever. Caring for him wasn't just a job anymore. It was family.

William stood by the hearth, sleeves rolled to his elbows as he adjusted logs on the fire. His gaze caught hers for a moment before he turned to help Ella hang another home-made ornament on the tree. Rose bustled from the kitchen with a tray of steaming cider, pressing mugs into Abby's and Carson's hands.

"Now it's Christmas," Rose declared, settling herself with a satisfied sigh and a tender look at Gramps. Abby wondered if something had sparked between the two adults who had become like grandparents to Carson.

The evening unfolded in a whirl of carols, cookies, and laughter. Carson and Ella sprawled on the rug, faces bright as they played with new toys. Gramps dozed with a blanket pulled over his knees, and Rose told stories of Christmases long ago while William listened, his smile soft and private.

Abby caught herself standing in the kitchen doorway, watching. It felt surreal. The kind of gathering she'd once thought was lost to her forever.

Later, as the festivities wound down, she and William washed dishes side by side in the kitchen. Steam curled from the sink, and the clatter of plates punctuated their silence.

"You didn't have to do this," William said, nodding toward the stack she was drying.

"Old habits," Abby replied, drying her hands. "Did Andy get settled in his new place?"

Officer Andy Reuben recently transferred to better job in a bigger city. Abby knew he and William had become close friends and was concerned about the hole this might leave in William's life.

"He did," William said. "He also said if you wanted to apply at the Chenaniah River police station and fill the vacancy, he'd put a good word in for you."

She chuckled. It surprised her to realize she had no desire to return to police work. It had been thrilling and invigorating, but she loved the quiet life she was able to lead taking care of Gramps and Carson. "I think I'll stick to home-based care."

He studied her for a moment. "Thank you."

She tilted her head. "For what? Turning down the opportunity to return to policing?"

"For staying. For Gramps. For Ella. For Carson." His voice was low, almost rough. "For all of us."

Her throat tightened. She wanted to tell him she hadn't stayed out of obligation, but because she had finally found a place she belonged. Instead, she gave him a small smile. "You don't have to thank me."

Ella burst into the room then, tugging at both their hands. "Stockings! Gramps said we can do stockings!"

The spell broke, and Abby followed Ella back to the fire, where Rose, Carson, and Gramps were already waiting with eager eyes.

Hours later, when the last song was sung, Abby and Carson walked back across the orchard to the cottage. The stars glittered brightly above, and the snow squeaked beneath their boots. Carson leaned against her, heavy with sleep, his mittened hand tucked in hers.

Inside, she carried him to bed, smoothing the hair from his forehead as he murmured drowsily. She whispered a prayer of thanks, tucked the blanket under his chin, and kissed him softly.

Then she settled into the armchair by the fire, a mug of tea warming her palms. Through the frosted window, the glow of the main house shone steadily across the orchard. Gramps was safe there. Rose too. Ella asleep upstairs. And William—

Her chest tightened. William was likely still awake, tidying up or reading by the fire.

For the first time in a long time, Abby let herself breathe deeply. She wasn't alone. She had Carson. She had a place. She had community.

And maybe—someday—she might have more. But for tonight, this was enough.

THE MAIN HOUSE was finally quiet. The fire burned low, and Rose had retired upstairs. Gramps snored softly in his chair with a blanket tucked around his shoulders. William stood at the window, watching Abby's shadow move about the cottage.

His chest ached at the sight. For months he had wrestled with guilt and fear, trying to keep Abby at arm's length. But tonight, watching her with Ella and Gramps, the battle ended.

Claire would always be a part of him, but she no longer needed him. Abby did. Carson did. Ella did. Gramps and Rose did. And, if he was honest, he needed them too.

He tugged at the wedding band still circling his finger, thumb brushing its rim. Then he let his hand fall to his side. It was time. Time to step out of yesterday's shadows and into the gift God had placed before him today.

"Still up?"

William turned. Gramps was blinking awake, eyes clearer than they'd been in weeks.

"Couldn't sleep," William admitted.

Gramps leaned forward. "You're thinking about her."

William didn't ask who he meant.

"You're allowed to," Gramps said softly. "Claire's gone. But you're still here. And so is Abby. Don't waste the second chance God's given you."

The words sank deep, loosening something long bound in William's chest. He turned to face the man who was more like a father than a grandfather. "Have you taken your own advice?"

A playful smile turned up the corners of the elderly man's lips. "Rose and I have talked about our future. She's not going anywhere."

William grinned. "I'm glad, Gramps. Really glad."

"It's your turn." He nodded once more toward the

cottage. "Don't let another day go by without telling her what she means to you."

William pulled on his coat and slipped his hand into his pocket. Rubbing his fingers over the velvet box. "I won't."

William stepped outside. The crunch of his boots carried him toward the cottage.

Abby met him at the door, her brows lifting in surprise. "Everything all right?"

"Better than all right." His throat tightened, suddenly overwhelmed by all this woman had come to mean to him.

She stepped aside, letting him in. The fire flickered low in the hearth, casting shadows across the small room.

Without bothering to take off his jacket, he took Abby's hand in his. "You've given this family hope again. You've given me hope again. I don't want you and Carson ever to wonder if you belong here."

Her breath hitched.

He reached into his pocket and drew out the small box he had carried for weeks, waiting for courage. Flipping it open, he showed her the ring inside. The diamond wasn't large, but it caught the firelight and shimmered between them.

He dropped to one knee. "I love you. I love Carson as if he were my own. And I love the way you love Ella, Rose, Gramps, and me. Abby Sinclair—will you marry me?"

Tears spilled down her cheeks as she pressed a hand to her mouth. For a heartbeat, the only sound was the soft pop of the fire.

"Yes," she whispered, voice trembling. "Yes."

Relief surged through him, fierce and certain. He slipped the ring onto her finger and then drew her into his arms. She rested her cheek against his chest, and he felt the fullness of God's love for him.

For the first time since Claire's passing, William felt whole. Not because he had forgotten her, but because he had chosen to live again. He pulled back just far enough to look down at Abby. When her face lifted to his, he pressed the most tender kiss against her lips.

Abby, Carson, Ella, Gramps, and Rose. They weren't pieces of his life—they were his life.

And this was only the beginning.

FATAL HOMECOMING
RETURN TO CHENANIAH RIVER

In the crosshairs of a killer...

Return to Chenaniah River with travel writer, Jessie Berns. Jessie returns to her hometown to find answers about her brother's suspicious death. With the help of an old friend, Detective Rick Chandler, they pursue a truth that someone is willing to do anything to keep hidden—even kill again. They uncover decades-old secrets that expose hidden sins and threaten the lifestyles of high-powered people in their small community. As they close in on the devious mastermind manipulating the town, it becomes frighteningly clear to Rick that Jessie is not the one calling the shots in her private investigation. She is the killer's new target.

PRAISE FOR FATAL HOMECOMING

If you are looking for a great read, encompassing Christian values, that will keep you spell bound from beginning to end, this is the book for you! It has a riveting plot that will keep you on the edge of your seat, with your heart pounding!! My attention was grabbed on the first page and I just could not put this book down. This book is packed full of suspense.

A great novel packed full of romance and suspense! Don't miss it!

—— ~KARLA / BOOK REVIEWER / 5 STARS

Wow - You are not going to put this one down until you are finished! If you enjoyed those Nancy Drew and Hardy Boy style books, this one is for you.

After many years away from the small town she grew up in, Jessie returns for the funeral of her brother. What happens after she arrives is nonstop action until the murderer or perhaps murderers are caught. I must admit, there were several characters that I suspected, but I certainly was way off base. The author has done a fabulous job of keeping the reader in the dark right up to the end. The lesson learned from the pile of rocks was important for all generations.

—— ~BETTY / BOOK REVIEWER / 5 STARS

Fatal Homecoming is a fast-paced suspense with more than enough action and danger to keep even the most avid suspense fan glued to its pages. I really enjoyed reading about the Royal Canadian Mounted Police for a change of pace.

Well rounded characters and a riveting plot keep me reading until the end. I also liked the way the author managed to weave a strong spiritual message into the story through conversations between the primary characters who found that depending on God was all that would get them through the increasing threats to their lives.

—— ~ PAM / DAYLONG REFLECTIONS / 5 STARS

ACKNOWLEDGMENTS

First things first: my writing crew. Karen, Sandy, Sandra, Tara, Darlene, Helena, Sara, Melanie, and Melony, you are the idea-wranglers, the plot-untanglers, and the "what if we..." dream team that turns chaos into an actual story. Our group has an insane ability to take a spark and turn it into a bonfire of a book. I'm lucky (and slightly terrified) to be part of it.

Rick, you lent me your policing expertise, and any mistakes are mine, not yours. (Let's be honest, if a police chief ever reads this, they'll probably call *me* in for questioning.)

Missy and Amanda, your enthusiasm and positivity keeps me writing. "Thank you" feels too small, but it's all I've got... and the next coffee is on me.

Jessica and Sandra, you brave souls read the earliest version of this book. Truly, that is an act of friendship. You endure typos, half-baked subplots, and characters who haven't quite decided who they want to be. You deserve medals. Or at least chocolate.

And to you, dear reader, thank you for picking up *Critical Care*. If you laughed, cried, or stayed up past bedtime, then I did my job. When you're ready for more, book 2, *Fatal Homecoming* is waiting with new chaos, drama, and—spoiler—romance.

ABOUT THE AUTHOR

Stacey Weeks writes contemporary romance and romantic suspense filled with strong women, honorable men, and just enough heart-pounding sweetness to keep you turning pages. Her stories are rooted in hope and grace.

She's also the author of non-fiction titles like *Glorious Surrender*, *Chasing Holiness*, *Season of Wonder*, and *Unceasing Prayer*. Stacey holds graduate certificates in Women's Ministry and Biblical Counselling from Heritage College and Seminary.

facebook.com/writerSWeeks

x.com/writerSWeeks

instagram.com/writersweeks

YOU CAN MAKE A DIFFERENCE

REVIEW CRITICAL CARE

Did you enjoy this book? You can make a difference. Honest reviews of books bring them to the attention of other readers. If you enjoyed this book, I would be grateful if you could spend a few minutes to leave an online review.

- Goodreads
- Bookbub

www.ingramcontent.com/pod-product-compliance
Lightning Source LLC
Chambersburg PA
CBHW071432260626
47170CB00008B/2684